I0542181

OPERATOR 5:
INVASION OF THE CRIMSON DEATH CULT

SECRET SERVICE #5™

AMERICA'S UNDERCOVER ACE

INVASION OF THE CRIMSON DEATH CULT

By Curtis Steele

STEEGER BOOKS • 2020

© 1935, 2020 Argosy Communications, Inc. All rights reserved.
Authorized and produced under license.

PUBLISHING HISTORY

"Invasion of the Crimson Death Cult" originally appeared in the September, 1935 (Vol. 5, No. 2) issue of *Operator #5* magazine. Copyright © 2020 by Argosy Communications, Inc. All rights reserved.

ALL RIGHTS RESERVED

No part of this book may be reproduced or utilized in any form or by any means, electronic or mechanical, without permission in writing from the publisher.

This edition has been marked via subtle changes, so anyone who reprints from this collection is committing a violation of copyright.

Visit STEEGERBOOKS.COM for more books like this.

CHAPTER 1
MOCKING THUNDER

THE WINDING Rio Grande lay silvered under the glow of a shell moon—a thin line of yellow mud marking the boundary between two nations; a frontier which, tonight, was being silently watched, jealously guarded.

A man in forest-green uniform crouched behind a weather-rotted fence peering at the soggy river bed. Yards away, another uniformed man stood warily behind the corner of a ramshackle shed also watching the snaky yellow curves that marked the course of the Rio. A third huddled behind a clump of cacti; a fourth lay flat behind a sand hill; still others formed an invisible line across the wasteland. Scores of them—all members of the ever-alert United States Border Patrol—peered warily across dry banks at the looming, border hills of Mexico.

They were awaiting a signal....

The officer, who stood ready to flash the signal, gazed intently at his radium-dialed watch. His lieutenants were grouped around him, beside the olive-drab sedan which had crawled silently toward the international border through the dim glow of the moon. Only a single, hard-packed, sand road led through this stretch of desert. In all the miles of arid waste which flanked the United States side of the Rio, there was not a glimmer of light, not a single flutter of movement; yet tonight, the Border Patrol was holding a grim guard along that line.

1

Captain Brennock had ordered the sentries to their unseen posts, yet even he did not know what to expect. He had executed cryptic commands received that same day from the Chief of

Fear and worship of Kasma became widespread as church after church was destroyed!

the Immigration Service—without knowing the reason behind them. He had been instructed to await a special investigator at this designated spot, but so far, no one had approached to

explain the urgent orders. Brennock, still peering at the luminous face of his watch, paced impatiently back and forth along the wind-packed sand.

"Damned if I know what's behind this!" he growled at his under-officers. "The border's as quiet as a tomb tonight." The sepulchral hush of the wasteland was disturbed abruptly by a throaty, drumming sound. Captain Brennock peered into the glowing sky. He discerned a black smudge moving against the star-spotted zenith—a plane circling downward. While it still hovered high, the throbbing of its exhaust faded away. Except for a faint whistling of wind past airfoils, there was no indication now that a plane was swooping toward the desert. It was weaving down dead-stick.

"Here comes our special investigator," Captain Brennock commented wryly. "Whoever the devil *he* may be!"

The lightless plane circled low above the Rio, then leveled over the lone road. Its fat tires crunched on the sand; Its brakes halted it directly behind the official sedan. Two passengers legged over the cowling of the observation-pit. Captain Brennock marched stiffly toward them, stopped short in consternation....

The captain was a veteran in the service which guarded the international line. He was a vital unit of the small army which patrolled the border from Corpus Christi, Texas, to San Ysidro, California. His was an important part of the gigantic task of policing the sixteen-hundred miles of boundary against smuggling operations of all kinds. He was not accustomed to yielding his command to any special investigator whom Washington might choose to send.

And certainly he was not at all eager to accept orders from anyone like these two passengers descending from the light-less plane.

"Captain Brennock?" the taller of the pair asked briskly.

HE WAS in his early twenties, clean-cut, sharp-eyed, garbed in carefully tailored civilian clothing. He was thoroughly American—a young man whom the captain thought might belong on a college campus, but not in this dangerous desert land as a special emissary of the Immigration Service. Brennock stared in astonishment and asked frostily: "Are *you*—?"

"I came as quickly as possible, Captain," the young man said crisply. "A non-stop flight from Washington. I'm glad I'm not too late."

His square hand drew a silver case from his vest-pocket as he spoke. His thumb-nail touched a secret spring; a metal leaf opened. Brennock's eyes sharpened as he read, in the bright moonlight, a letter framed inside the case. His stern brows arched in surprise.

THE WHITE HOUSE
Washington

To Whom It May Concern:

The identity of the bearer of this letter must be kept strictly confidential.

He is Operator 5 of the United States Intelligence Service.

The signature affixed to the credential was that of the President of the United States.

James Christopher closed the case with a click, restored it to his pocket while the captain stared.

"My friend, Tim Donovan," he introduced. "Too young to be an accredited member of the service, Captain, but an extremely competent lad. He's my unofficial assistant."

Jimmy Christopher's companion grinned broadly at Captain Brennock's discomfiture. He was tough, Irish, in his teens. His appearance—a freckled face and pug nose shadowed by a broken-billed cap, a well-knit body covered with hard-worn coat and knickers—belied his talents. He had worked courageously with Operator 5 on many vital cases, and his help had been of the greatest importance. His broad grin grew as Captain Brennock mumbled in confusion:

"You—you are to take command here?"

"Not at all, Captain," Jimmy Christopher answered with a slow smile. "You will command. I came to explain the great importance of our task tonight—and to take charge of any prisoners we may capture."

"Prisoners?" the captain echoed. "I'd like to know what the devil is up!"

"Tonight," Operator 5 explained, "one of the most daring alien-smuggling operations in the history of our country will be attempted." He removed his wallet, took a folded paper from it, extended the paper to Brennock. "That, Captain, may explain."

The captain peered puzzled at cryptic symbols:

ENJOU ADHUYB NALORG CRAHYT CVZXW....

OPERATOR 5 gazed across the undulated wasteland. He

appreciated the magnitude of the Border Patrol's task. Its scattered stations must deploy the limited number of men along the long line while daring, organized bands of smugglers strove desperately to outwit them. When, during the dry season, the eight-hundred miles of Rio Grande became only a band of mud, easily crossed, the ordeal of the men in forest-green uniform became even greater. Low water and darkness were enemies which connived with the criminal gangs who relentlessly operated across the international line." *

Captain Brennock blurted: "I can't make head or tail of this thing! It's a cipher message, isn't it?"

"A message written in one of the cleverest cipher systems yet devised," Jimmy Christopher agreed. "The translation is on the second page. I worked over those symbols, Captain, for forty-eight hours at a stretch before I found the secret."

While the captain read, Operator 5 studied the hard faces of the officers around Brennock. Their skins were baked crust-hard by the blasting, desert winds. Their arduous, nerve-straining work kept them lean and hard-muscled. They were plainsmen,

---

* AUTHOR'S NOTE: Uncle Sam's watch upon our borders means that our border patrolmen must patrol a total of 15,000,000 miles a year while seeking to stem the tide of illegal entries. They number 2,000 men and keep their vigil day and night along both borders. Within a period of a year they question 1,000,000 people crossing the borders, examine half a million automobiles, and besides vast amounts of contraband, seize 25,000 aliens and smugglers. The average citizen of the United States does not dream of the vast, quiet war waging along our borders at all times.

diplomats, shrewd detectives, every one of them—and theirs was a uniform which never had been dishonored.

"This," Captain Brennock exclaimed impatiently, "means no more to me than the first!"

The message was indeed, baffling:

HUMBLE GREETINGS TO THE SON OF KASMA—YOUR DEVOUT IN THE SERVICE OF CONVERSION BEGS TO HONOR HIMSELF BY REPORTING THE ADVENT OF WORSHIPFUL FOLLOWERS THIS THIRD NIGHT—HUNDREDS THEY NUMBER AND THEY AWAIT THE PROTECTION OF KASMA FOR THEIR DANGEROUS PASSAGE FROM CATALTUL-QUE INTO THE LAND OF GREAT PROMISE—OUR FAITH FOLLOWS THE MIGHT OF KASMA AND GROWS STRONG AT THE TOUCH OF THE HAND OF THE SON OF KASMA—POWER FOR-EVER—BAI

"Cataltulque," Operator 5 asked quietly, "lies directly across the border in Mexico, doesn't it? It has been used before as an alien-running station—but never on such a daring scale as is planned for tonight. 'Hundreds,' that message says, Captain. It can mean only that there is a gigantic scheme to run a horde of aliens into the United States before dawn—Orientals, without a doubt."

Brennock blurted: "Impossible! That many aliens could never reach Cataltulque without our knowing it. If this message is the reason for my orders, you've sent my men out on a fool's errand—a wild goose chase! You're—"

"Rain!"

THE SINGLE word, blurted in surprise, brought silence. The soft spatter of the first drops to fall from the night sky had escaped Brennock's notice. The many years he had spent in the desert, in the Immigration Service, had taught him that, at this season, the ground

lay scorched under cloudless skies; that for months the aridity would continue unbroken. Yet now, as he stared, rain fell—and the few drops became a quickening sprinkle.

"Not a cloud in the sky!"

"This never happened before!"

Brennock gazed around in bewilderment a moment, then shrugged and turned back to Jimmy Christopher. Even while he spoke, the rainfall became heavier—a downpour pelting out of a clear sky, whipping across the rolling sand hills, lashing over the startled men.

"I put no stock in this secret message of yours," the captain growled candidly. "What does it mean? What's this thing that's mentioned several times—Kasma?"

With bewildering swiftness the rain was growing heavier—in the glow of an unobscured moon! Through the swish and the spatter, Operator 5's answer came quietly:

"The full explanation of that message, Captain, I confess I do not know. But I'm absolutely certain of its importance. You may be interested in learning how I found it. Because it is my work,

I recently took to trailing an Oriental alien known to be a mystic—one named Zarin. I intercepted an airmail letter addressed to him, and found the cipher message."

"Well?" Brennock demanded, peering around through the sluicing rain. "God, I don't understand this! A damned cloudburst in the middle of the dry season!"

"I consider the message important enough, Captain," Operator 5 said quietly, "to place Zarin under arrest. He is being held now. He has refused to speak one word; he is contemptuously

defiant. It was I who asked the cooperation of the Immigration Service for this detail tonight and I—"

A sudden, sluicing deluge muffled Operator 5's words. The drenching downpour forced the Border Patrol officers to retreat into their cars. Captain Brennock turned suddenly, tramped over softening sand, sloshed through puddles, and huddled against the side of his sedan. The cold torrent became even thicker as Operator 5 quickly followed with Tim Donovan. Already they were soaked to the skin—and the rain was becoming a blinding cataract.

"If you still doubt me, Captain," Jimmy Christopher shouted through the loudening ripple of the rain, "look across the Rio now! What's that? What are those lights?"

"I'll be damned!" Brennock blurted, staring in dismay, "there's somebody coming across!"

"Hundreds!" Operator 5 quoted grimly. "Hundreds whose 'faith follows the might of Kasma!'"

They peered in consternation through the sheeting rain. Now it was blotting out the surrounding wilderness, though the moon continued to shine through it with a silvery glow. It was waving, wet drapery drawing closer around the men who stared in bewilderment, their faces streaming. Through the deluge, they saw diffused gleams—lights moving on the hills beyond the Rio. Scores of the swinging sparkles appeared as the amazed men of the Border Patrol peered.

"Flash your signal, Captain!" Operator 5 ordered sharply. "Flash it unless you wish those hundreds of fanatical aliens to cross the line!"

THE FURY of the rain washed over the desert land and beat with a cosmic wrath upon the men in the road. Brennock, for one stunned moment after Jimmy Christopher's command, could not move. Bewildered by the drops lashing into his face, he jerked up a Verey pistol, raised it high. He touched the trigger and a gleaming red ball streaked through the drenching rain. Across the pouring sand hills, the scarlet light flashed its signal.

The mystified men of the Border Patrol shivering in the sharp coldness of the downpour, saw the flash and sprang from their hiding places. Ducking low, holding service guns that streamed water, peering at the flickering lights across the Rio, they advanced through a torrent that almost robbed them of their senses.

11

When the crimson signal flared through the sluicing rain, Operator 5 turned quickly back to the plane. "With me, Tim!" he commanded as he ran. Beneath one wing of the swift Army pursuit, the pilot was crouching to escape the Niagara pouring from the sky. Operator 5's hand shot to the lieutenant's shoulder:

"We're going up!"

"What?" The pilot stared in blank astonishment. "Go up in this storm? I wouldn't be able to see. We'd be forced down—a crack up! We can't go up in this rain! It's suicide, sir!"

Operator 5 turned sharply. "In the pit, Tim!" he commanded; and he reached for the cowling of the fore-cubby. The amazed boy scrambled in as Jimmy Christopher grasped the crank. Rain whipped across them; their clothing streamed water; the lashing drops sprayed into their faces with blinding thickness. Operator 5 twisted the motor into snorting action.

"For God's sake, don't go up!" The pilot screamed, backing out into the downpour. "You'll crack! I tell you, you'll crack!"

The roar of the motor was Jimmy Christopher's answer. He ducked low behind the windshield, threw off the brakes, felt the trucks crunch through soggy sand. Desperately, he swerved to avoid the official car; then he opened the throttle wide. The wings trailed water, the propeller spun a rainbow in the moonlight, as Jimmy Christopher hurled the swift pursuit into the air.

While he circled up, with cold drops striking his face like lead shots, he narrowed his eyes against the fury and peered overside. The twinkling lights near the Rio were now moving rapidly. Each sparkling spot was separated from the others, and the gleams revealed weird running figures. They were struggling across the yellow mud of the river, climbing the banks on the United States side, darting across the streaming sand hills. Orange flashes told Operator 5 that the guns of the Border Patrol were hurling a leaden defiance to the cordons of aliens.

Climbing steeply, Operator 5 forced the plane to its limit; and he felt the downpour slacken as he rose. Though the drops still beat upon him and Tim with cold fury, they thinned as he spiraled. Abruptly he was shuttling through clear air, far above the international line. And he looked down on an amazing sight.

Below the plane, the rain was still spilling in a tumult that was flooding the desert! The glistening mass of falling water was surrounded by miles of spreading sand on which no drop had fallen! Over all the wasteland, the moon beamed, even upon the area visited by the mysterious storm—the spot where the sentries of the Border Patrol had rushed into action! So thick was the torrent beneath Operator 5 that he could see nothing of the green-uniformed men. Only a faint glimmer of lights, the dim flashing of gun-flame, told him that within the flooded area a battle was being fought.

"Jimmy!" The startled cry came from the rear pit. "Do you feel it?"

OPERATOR 5 had straightened alertly in the pit. His sensitive nerves had registered a warning an instant before the Irish lad had called. His body was filled now with a sensation such as he had never felt before. It was a strange numbness, a creeping paralysis that affected his whole being—a rising sense of confusion. Suddenly Operator 5 felt that his body was useless, that his mind was disintegrating, that he was flying through cosmic space into the eternal emptiness between the stars.

"Jimmy! Up—there!"

Operator 5 sensed a note of terror in Tim Donovan's voice, but the strange lethargy still held him. The mere raising of his eyes, to peer into the zenith in response to Tim's call, was an effort. He was a dream creature, moving with leaden slowness, weighted with an unfeeling torpidity, incapable of thought.

Yet Jimmy Christopher forced himself to look up. He saw Tim pointing into the reaches of the night sky—holding up one hand as though it was a leaden thing. Turning his eyes still higher drained him of strength. He sat lax, feeling no desire to move the controls, unmindful of the disaster which continued negligence must inevitably bring. Like an automaton, he stared into the sky.

It was cloudless. The moon was a blinding silver spot, and beyond it, the stars were glittering points. Yet there was something else—something hovering in the zenith—a thing like a strange insect crawling across the studded ceiling of the sky. Operator 5 peered at it as the lethargy he felt began to give way to a mad delirium.

Desperately, he hardened his hand on the stick as a confusion like insanity swept over his mind. With torturous effort, he kicked the rudders, realizing with frantic hysteria that unless he kept control of the plane it would crash into the wastes of the desert. The threat of death brought strength to him that defied the strange spell. He hurled the pursuit upward, squinting at the tiny thing hovering above, climbed toward it under full power.

Beneath him the rain was still pouring. All around, dry desert spread under the gleam of the moon. Above—what?

While the plane roared upward, another warning cry came from Tim Donovan. The pursuit veered, teetered, as a force enveloped it. It was at first a slight tremor only faintly different from the note of the motor; but it became a violent quaking that shook the crate from boss to tail. Instant by instant, the craft's vibration increased, until it was waggling through the air like a creature caught helpless in the teeth of a gigantic wild sky-dog.

The savage shaking of the plane was threatening to rip it apart in mid-air! That danger made Operator 5 work at the controls with renewed desperation. The ship responded erratically as he kicked it out of its climb, sent it plunging low across dry sand-hills. The strange numbness still filled his mind, yet a single thought dominated him—a mad desire to escape that unknown power.

The earth twisted in front of him. The horizon rocked like a see-saw in spite of all Operator 5's efforts to dress the ship. The ground was a blinding blur, a confusion in which death lurked—a promise of a crash that would transform the pursuit into a mass of splintered wreckage. With all his draining strength, Jimmy Christopher strove to fling the ship away from that danger....

SUDDENLY THE strange force vanished. For a long, breathless minute the plane still quaked, but the violence of its tremors diminished. As abruptly as the uncanny effects had struck upon Operator 5, they passed away. Now the world lay solid below him, the sky spread clear above. In the zenith, there was no hint of the power that had struck; but beyond, near the border, a torrent of rain was still pouring....

Jimmy Christopher drove his plane toward it. When the first drops whisked past the slipstream, he shuttled the crate low to the road. As he prepared to land, a swift change came over the storm-torn terrain. The rumble of the rain grew softer. The torrent became a mere spatter as suddenly as though a gigantic faucet in the sky had been turned off, the downpour ended!

As the air cleared, Jimmy Christopher gazed across the area it had flooded. The road was a running stream; puddles had collected between the hills because the rain had fallen more rapidly than the sand could soak it up. From the Rio beyond came a steady ominous roar as draining water sped like a wall down the muddy bed. The last drop fell—and at that moment, a thunder-clap shook heaven and earth together.

No flash of lightning preceded it. The deafening burst of sound struck out of the sky the moment the rain ended. It made the earth tremble; it rolled in rumbling echoes into the distance, and was gone. Yet it was not thunder. It was laughter—laughter that roared out of the spaces between the worlds as though from the throat of a gloating god—laughter that mocked!

The thunderous burst of mirth brought a hush over the earth—moments of dismayed silence....

Operator 5 sprang out of the pit of the plane; he ran rapidly along the road with Tim Donovan following. Their clothing still streamed. As he sprinted, Jimmy Christopher peered around and saw no glimmer of light among the hills, no flashing of guns of the green-uniformed corps. He found Captain Brennock standing in drenched uniform, staring dazed across the wastes.

Operator 5 stood by while a breathless lieutenant stumbled to a stop, gasped a report: "Gibson and Wright, sir—dead! God knows what killed them—there're no marks! Dropped dead in their tracks sir—"

A second man, pulling himself to a breathless stop, interrupted. "Before God—a dozen men are lost in the river! It hit them all together, sir; swept them along! They can't get out of that flood—

not now, sir! They're drowned like rats. When it hit them, they—they didn't seem to even try to get away from it!"

"Hunter! Hunter, sir!" a third man exclaimed. He had run up through the sticky sand; he leaned exhausted against the sedan as he blurted his report. "He's gone mad! He's—gone—mad!"

A wild, strangling scream tore out of the night. It shrilled across the sand hills and brought an icy chill to the men who heard it. Peering across pools of water that were sinking into the porous ground, Operator 5 saw a man running, stumbling, swaying, scrambling over hills, fleeing from an unseen danger with exhausting desperation. He fell, scrambled up, ran wildly again—and screamed. It was the cry of a destroyed mind—a cry of abject terror....

THE MEN on the road stood motionless until the fleeing figure vanished in the distance, until the choking cries vanished on the wind. Appalled, Captain Brennock snapped: "Go after Hunter! Get him!" As two of his bewildered lieutenants ran into the moonlight, he turned to glare at Jimmy Christopher.

"You heard that! My men killed—God knows how! Drowned in this damnable flood! Turned into raving maniacs! What in God's name happened?" He rushed on. "They got across—those damned aliens! Where are they now? God only knows! But they got across, all of them—all of them!"

Jimmy Christopher said quietly: "They are only a small part of an army which has already entered our country, Captain. They will be followed by hundreds of others—thousands—all instruments of a devilish power. What we've seen tonight means that the power fears nothing!"

Quietly one of Brennock's lieutenants said: "They all got across—except one, Captain. We've taken a prisoner."

Two drenched men were leading the prisoner toward the captain's car. Between them, a strange figure moved in the moonlight. It seemed to be neither man nor woman—a being that could not belong to the human race—though it walked upright. It seemed shapeless, grotesque; the two men who accompanied it brought it to a stop in front of Captain Brennock. The officer stared.

It was a fat figure, with great thick arms, but without legs, without feet or hands. Its head was a huge peaked formation on its immensely thick shoulders. Staring, Jimmy Christopher saw that it was scarlet. He stepped forward; his hands touched the being; and he withdrew with a tight smile.

"There is no cause for wonder," he said tersely. "This man is wearing a very thick garment. There are, you see, eyeholes in the helmet."

Brennock was staring at the creature's eyes. They were deep, conical depressions in the grotesque, peaked head—two funnel-shaped hollows, at the bottom of which black eyeballs gleamed. Operator 5, while Brennock watched, fastened his fingers in the softness of this creature's head. He pulled, and a thick, crimson helmet came away in his grasp. Seemingly absurdly small, the uncovered face of a man became visible on the tremendously broad shoulders—a saffron face, from which black, slanted eyes gleamed.

Brennock snapped: "Get him out of that thing!"

The two officers snatched at the strange garment, jerked it over the Oriental's head. Operator 5 took it, and saw that it was soft and light, though several inches thick. Its wearer stood revealed now—a slight figure, garbed in silken, Oriental costume. Brennock glared at the Yellowese grimly, snapped:

"What's your name? Where did you come from? Why were you wearing that damned thing? Where are the others that came across with you? Do you hear me? Answer my questions! Who brought you across the border?"

The prisoner remained mute.

"You're under arrest—do you understand that?" Brennock stormed. "Under arrest for illegal entry. You're subject to deportation under the law. Unless you want to rot in jail, you'll answer my questions now. Who's behind all this?"

The prisoner said nothing. Operator 5 spoke quietly to the captain: "This man is no ordinary Yellowese. He is of high caste.

But, whoever he is, he is now a prisoner of the Intelligence. We will hold him. Questioning him now will get you nowhere. Zarin—whom I trailed in New York—has not uttered a single word since his capture. But—"

He stepped closer. The prisoner's almond eyes turned blackly upon Jimmy Christopher. They were lighted by extreme self-confidence; they burned with a zealous faith; they were filled with a cool contempt. The quiet question which Operator 5 asked brought a fiercer intensity behind that dark gleam.

"Who is the power you worship?"

The answer was a whisper of one word, a word that expressed fanatical devotion, an undying faith; it was followed by an unbroken and serene silence, as though this man were determined never to speak another name. It brought a chill to Operator 5's heart—the same dread he had felt when mocking, thunderous laughter had rolled out of the sky:

"Kasma!"

CHAPTER 2
"KASMA STRIKES!"

THE CLEAR, bright, warm morning was appropriate to the Seventh Day and the worship of God. Church bells had pealed their call to devotion over New York City, and congregations had gathered. The rich and the humble had come together in the great Church of the Divine on Riverside Drive, and the mighty organ had poured forth its song of praise. Now, as the hand of the minister raised, the words of a prayer brought a hush over the bowed heads.

Outside the portals of the tremendous church, a heavy car drew to the curb. It paused directly at the entrance of the famed edifice, but its door did not open; no one alighted from it. It remained motionless, curtains drawn. Through a slit, slanted eyes peered at the facade of the noble structure. One moment it gazed upon this House of God; then it vanished.

Two other cars turned from the side-street, braked near the corner. Both were powerful sedans; both were units in the automobile fleet which, without identifying mark of any kind, were used by the far-flung United States Intelligence Service. In the fore-seat of the first, beside the agent known as C-6, a young man and a boy sat alertly. They were Operator 5 and Tim Donovan.

"Keep the motor running, C-6" Jimmy Christopher directed quietly. "Watch that car. The devil only knows what they're up to, but we've got to be prepared for anything."

C-6 answered tightly: "Right! Is—is this connected in any way with Z-7's information? I've run up against plenty of tough propositions before, and I've always managed to keep my head, but this is getting me. Is—is this connected with—?"

C-6 broke off as Operator 5 drew a yellow flimsy from his pocket. It was a message which had reached him only that morning from the director of all activities of the United States Intelligence, Z-7. He read it again, solemnly, while Tim Donovan alertly watched the car ahead—the car with the drawn blinds:

... SPECIAL ATTENTION OPERATOR 5... INEX-PLICABLE CASUALTIES OCCURRING WITHIN INTELLIGENCE SERVICE... SCORE OF AGENTS AFFECTED IN NEW YORK CITY ALONE... TWO OPERATORS FOUND WANDERING, HUNGRY. VICTIMS OF COMPLETE AMNESIA... FIVE OTHERS AFFLICTED WITH SAME LOSS OF MEMORY IN LOCAL HOSPITALS AS RESULT OF ACCIDENT OR EXPOSURE... SIX OTHERS DISAPPEARED, NO TRACE YET FOUND... FOUR FOUND DEAD WITH NO CLUE THOUGH DEATH WAS NOT NATURAL... THREE MAD AND NOW IN CONFINEMENT... REPORTS FROM SUB-HEADQUARTERS INDICATE SAME CONDITION IN OTHER CITIES... SERVICE BEING DECIMATED BUT WE HAVE NO INKLING AS TO CAUSE—INVESTIGATION IMPERATIVE... Z-7....

The code symbol prefixed to this amazing message meant: *these orders take precedence over all others.*

"Whatever the connection is," Operator 5 said quietly, "it's our job to find it, C-6. This is a lead, I'm sure of it. I'm positive that the Orientals in that car are aliens who have smuggled themselves into the country—for a devilish purpose."

"Your prisoner—the Yellowese you captured at the border a few nights ago—" C-6 asked tensely, "he hasn't talked?"

"He has spoken only one word—*Kasma!*"

OPERATOR 5 stepped from the car with Tim Donovan; they glanced at the sedan with the blinded windows as they turned to the second Intelligence machine. Out of it came four men, each carrying small, black, leather cases. Jimmy Christopher directed them:

"Take your positions. Watch your indicators every moment. If there is a deflection, note the degree and try to fix the direction. That's highly important."

The four men—trusted agents of the Intelligence Service—walked quietly toward the church carrying the black cases. Two of them took positions at the doors; the two others circled to the rear of the edifice. Operator 5, when they had taken their posts, returned to the first service car. Tim Donovan tugged at his sleeve, asked:

"What is it you've planned, Jimmy? What are the boxes those men are carrying?"

"Galvanometers, Tim," Operator 5 explained. "Simple instruments sensitive enough to detect any electrical field or flux if they're brought close to it.* It's a stab in the dark, Tim, but—it may tell us something important."

---

* AUTHOR'S NOTE: Galvanometers are used for measuring small electrical currents, and there are several types. An ordinary compass will demonstrate to the reader the general principle of the galvanometer. Brought near a magnetic field, such as the housing of a motor in operation, the needle will

The boy was bewildered. He knew that, following Jimmy Christopher's swift return by plane from the international border, strange ideas had played in his mind. Operator 5 had been silent, preoccupied. Because neither of the Yellowese prisoners of the Service had spoken—the first named Zarin taken in New York and the second unknown seized at the border—Jimmy Christopher had resumed his hunt for Oriental aliens. He had followed leads day and night until, on this balmy Sunday morning, the trail had led him to the portals of a great church.

"I don't know what to make of it at all," the boy mused as he sat beside Operator 5 and watched the car with the drawn curtains. "The aliens coming over the border—the terrific rain in the middle of the dry season—and the force that hit us in the air. I thought I was losing my mind and—Jimmy!" Tim's eyes widened. "That's the connection you're working on! Some of our operators losing their memory and going crazy—and something like that happened to us while we were flying above the rain!"

Operator 5 had started up. He did not answer Tim's keen observation. He whispered tersely: "Watch that man!"

The door of the shaded sedan had opened. Out of it, a strange figure had stepped. The mere sight of him brought a startled gasp from C-6; it amazed Tim Donovan and fascinated even Operator 5. For the man who appeared in the bright sunshine was garbed in a silken robe and a silken, blood-red turban.

---

deflect. When placed near a wire carrying a direct current, the compass will indicate the direction of the flow of the current. Special galvanometers are made which are extremely sensitive.

He stood with serene confidence, facing the portals of the church, strikingly tall, his face lean, his hands with long claw-like nails folded within the flowing sleeves of his scarlet robe. He seemed to have a supreme disregard of his surroundings, of the few men and women on the sidewalk who paused to peer at him in amazement. His was a manner of complete confidence—a confidence so great it might be supported by a superhuman power—as he moved with slow, gliding steps toward the open doors of the church....

At the pulpit, within the consecrated walls the Reverend Richard Warren spread his arms in a gesture of supplication. His sonorous voice rang clear and strong.

"Over all this great nation, blessed from its birth, paganism has spread, now followed by the deeper darkness of infidel beliefs. We must not turn from God to the abyss of mysticism! We must keep our faith pure; we must hold the symbol of Christianity high above all other creeds—for, if we yield, we shall become lost to God. We shall—"

THE MINISTER'S earnest voice broke off as he peered along the aisle. He saw a flash of bright red—blood red—among the subdued colors of the church. He saw, standing erect just within the doors of his church, a being garbed in scarlet robe and scarlet turban. After a moment's confusion, the Reverend Warren resumed:

"I call upon you to fight down the evil forces that are striving to enslave you. There is but one God—the God we worship. There is no God before Him. We praise Him, and He showers His benefactions upon us. We have faith, and He blesses us. Without our trust in God, this nation might never have been founded. Without our faith, this nation will plunge into the black despair of fanaticism. I plead with you to fight it with all the strength of your souls, to battle it down so that our true faith may reign—"

Again the sincere voice of the minister faded into a hush. He had seen the crimson-robed figure move. He had watched the strange, tall man with the saffron skin advance with slow, gliding steps along the aisle toward his pulpit. The eyes of the congregation turned now toward the man in scarlet. Amid utter silence he

A section of the stone ceiling fell among the people, creating bedlam!

26

advanced, step by step; when he paused it was to raise aloft one lean, long-nailed hand.

"There is no faith but the worship of Kasma!"

His deep, intoning voice was like a whisper in the vastness of the church, yet it carried a power that preserved the silence. The clawed hand remained aloft; the black, slanting eyes turned gleaming upon the congregation. And again the fascinating whisper came, reaching across the spaciousness of the House of God.

"Kasma alone is the faith for the devout. Kasma created the world from nothingness. Kasma's breath is the breath of your lungs that ceases when he abandons you as an unbeliever. Kasma's is the universe to make and keep and destroy. His patience with the blind is at an end. To Kasma's own, he gives life; to those who doubt, he metes out death. The day of doom for the unbelievers is at hand.

"Kasma strikes!"

The eyes of the congregation kept upon the scarlet-robed figure with an awed fascination. From his pulpit, the outraged minister made a gesture of protest even while he stared in bewilderment at the ominous man who had whispered that sentence of doom. Ushers hurried down the aisle toward the red-cloaked man; but even as they moved, a sense of dread filled them—and an ominous rumble came to their ears.

The church was trembling. Through all its walls, a vibration passed, wringing groans and shudders from the beams, bringing a buzzing from the colored-glass windows, shaking even the altar where the minister stood. Moment by moment, the quaking of the church grew stronger while the man in the scarlet robe held one long-nailed hand uplifted.

The ushers stood spellbound, their intention of ejecting this weird figure forgotten. Men and women sprang from their pews in fear. Every eye turned as a fragment of glass fell, broken, from a window with a musical tinkle. Every heart speeded as the great edifice became a shaking shell. The entire church was trembling on its foundations and the violence of the disturbance was growing each second. Suddenly, scores of men and women leaped to their feet and rushed toward the doors.

The voice of the minister rang sharply through the tumult of stampeding feet, through the groaning of the wrenching walls.

"This man is an infidel! His is not the voice of God!"

"Kasma strikes!"

AT THE main entrance of the great church, Operator 5 hurried aside from the hundreds of men and women who were rushing into the street. They fled in silent terror, as though the awesome presence of the scarlet-robed one had stifled their voices. And as they rushed, the quaking of the church became a terrifying rumble that echoed through its every beam and stone. The floor rocked; the walls powdered out mortar; the hanging lights pendulumed; and the voice of the man of God on the pulpit was lost in a heavy crash.

Out of the wall above the altar, a great stone carving tumbled! It spilled down upon the pulpit even as the minister whirled in dismay. It rolled with ponderous power before the man, hand pressed hard to the huge Bible, could stir. It bounded upon him like a living thing eager to destroy! A cry of terror broke from his throat as the tremendous weight crushed upon him.

At that moment he died....

The crash of masonry struck fiercer terror into the hearts of the scattering congregation. Women screamed and men cried out hoarsely as they mobbed toward the doors. In the frantic crush, the infirm fell, and in their horror the strong trampled them. Mixed with the shouting and the shrieking was the frightened whimper of children swept helplessly into the unthinking mob. The congregation had come to worship; now it was fleeing in fear as a great church shook with a disintegrating force!

Again masonry crashed as a section of wall spilled down. A timber cracked from its supports in the ceiling and descended like a blunt blade upon those crowding, terrorized, through one yawning door. Shriller screams mingled with the crashing of stone as lives were crushed out beneath the deadly weight. The air gusted with the dust of crumbling mortar—and the whole church quaked under the destructive power that was upon it.

Operator 5 shouldered past scores who fled in terror and peered at the man in the scarlet robe. The crimson being was moving with slow, gliding step toward the crowded entrance. The scores who saw him forgot the danger threatening them, retreated in awe. The black, slanted eyes of the man gazed far away as he moved along the aisle that fearfully was opened to him. Jimmy Christopher alone was able to fight down the hypnotic fascination of this uncanny figure. He started forward, his one thought to take him a prisoner—but a frightened cry stopped him.

A great section of the stone ceiling dropped with a roar like an exploding cannon. Blinding dust clouded over broken pews, blanketing from sight those trapped by the plunging stone. In that frantic bedlam, Operator 5 heard the pitiful cries of children. He spun, groping through the choking dust, toward a small hand he saw reaching up from among the broken wood of a crushed pew. He struggled forward desperately while the entire shell of the church shook with an added violence, threatening to collapse any instant....

Jimmy Christopher tore broken wood aside, saw the widened eyes of a little five-year-old girl peering at him. A boy, slightly older, lay huddled beside her, speechless with terror. In childish fear, they had hidden beneath the pew at the first mad scramble; the dropping masonry had imprisoned them. Even while Operator 5 struggled to free them from the death-trap, mortar crumbled down and deafening crashes sounded around him.

He grasped the girl in his arms and the boy scrambled after him frantically as he groped through the dust-laden air. They stumbled down from the mound of broken stone as a woman rushed wildly toward them. She seized the girl in her arms and sobbed. The man at her side lifted the boy, frantically, and they hurried together toward the dust-clouded doorway. In their mad anxiety, they could think only of escaping the doom that was rocking the church on its foundations, of reaching the safety of the street beyond.

OPERATOR 5 pushed after them. He could not know how many victims were trapped in the fallen debris of the ceiling and walls; how many had already died. His rescue of the two children had forced him to turn from the man in the scarlet robe; but now he shouldered his way out into the street. The Drive was crowded with the hundreds who had fled from the doors of the church; they were running wildly, scattering. And among the dispersing crowd, a car was moving away.

It spurted as Jimmy Christopher ran to the first Intelligence machine. Tim Donovan reached out to grip his arm. "In that car, Jimmy! He's getting away in it!" Operator 5 saw, in the insane confusion, his four co-agents hurrying toward him with their black cases. The lid of each case was raised, disclosing a dial and a slender needle. Through the hubbub of the mob, the first reported:

"No deflection!"

"No deflection whatever!"

Operator 5 snapped: "Get away from this place! That church is coming down in a minute! Order these people away and clear out!" He peered appalled at the great edifice before he ducked into the car. Before his eyes, the whole structure was shaking as though with the violent tremors of an earthquake. The stone spires had already collapsed. The great dome was trembling on its base. The windows were shattered and gushing out billows of dust. Already the destructive power had wrought appalling havoc, but the ever-increasing violence of the force was threatening to make it an entire ruin.

"Get after that car!" Jimmy Christopher snapped. He ducked low into the Intelligence machine as C-6 meshed the gears. "Follow it!"

The sedan spurted from the curb, horn blaring, while frantic people, still running from the doomed edifice, scattered from its path. It streaked up the Drive while Operator 5 peered back in cold dismay. Tim Donovan's hand clutched his arm unconsciously; a gasp of utter bewilderment and grief broke from the boy's lips.

A crash louder than all the former ones enveloped the church. As if the destructive power was determined to end its work, an earth-jarring shock struck through the edifice. Its great dome plunged down. Its facade crumpled and spilled into the street. Its walls gave way, transformed into smoking masses of cracked stone. Far out into the street the broken bits avalanched, while screams and shouts filled the air, while scores died in the final disaster.

A few moments before the Church of the Divine had stood a majestic and inspiring house of worship; now it lay a heap of dust-shrouded wreckage!

A sharper chill filled Operator 5's heart as C-6 sent the sedan speeding up the Drive. Above the frantic crying of the terrorized crowd, a new sound rose. It came like a deafening clap of thunder, a burst that roared out of the bright and unclouded sky. Its rumbling din covered all the city—mocking laughter.

Kasma laughed!

The thunderous, mocking burst became scattering echoes that left behind an awed hush. Once the laughter of the destroying god sounded above the destruction wrought by its power; then it was gone. It silenced the cries of the stricken crowd; there was no sound now save the whisper of the Intelligence car as it sped. "It's ahead!"

OPERATOR 5 turned, at C-6's exclamation, and peered up the lane of streaming pavement. The sedan with the drawn blinds was traveling at amazing speed along the winding Drive that flanked the Hudson River. Beside it now, a second car was speeding, matching its velocity—a light truck. Operator 5 studied the rear of the truck as he urged C-6:

"Don't let it slip you. We want that man in the scarlet robe!"

C-6 pressed the accelerator to the floorboards; but suddenly, he straightened. An expression of bewilderment shone in his eyes. Operator 5 saw a startling laxness of C-6's features—a blankness like that on the face of an imbecile. He felt at the same time, within himself, that same deadening lethargy which had seized upon him while flying in the air above the international border. Desperately he summoned all his mental strength to combat the hypnotic paralysis as he forced himself to reach for the wheel.

One of his four men was in the rear seat. Glancing back, Jimmy Christopher saw that same expression of imbecility on G-9's face too. The secret agent was sitting torpidly, oblivious of his surroundings.

"Your galvanometer!" Operator 5 snapped. "Look at it! Read it!"

G-9's eyes dropped slowly. He peered at the dial of the sensitive instrument and his gaze rose heavily again. He said in a far-away whisper: "No deflection. No—deflection!"

"Watch the car!" The frenzied cry came from Tim Donovan. "You're heading—"

The crash that followed was more violent to Jimmy Christopher's senses than those which had caused the disintegration of the great church. The roar that sounded in his ears was even more deafening than the burst of mocking laughter that had sounded out of cosmic space. He knew only vaguely that the sedan, rushing at top speed, had jounced over the curb and had hurtled against a building front. The car wrenched in a death spasm—and blackness covered Jimmy Christopher's world.

OPERATOR 5 felt a hand shaking him, as the darkness began to recede after a timeless interval. He felt sunlight shining through his closed lids, stinging his eyeballs. With a tremendous effort, he brought himself to a sitting position, blinked through a bleary haze.

An ambulance was drawn up to the curb. Uniformed policemen were holding a crowd back, and two men in white uniform were at Jimmy Christopher's side. A cut on his forehead burned as he gazed at the sprawled body of C-6. Another man in starched uniform was crouched over the secret agent. He rose, and Operator 5 heard him say solemnly: "Dead."

"Tim!" Operator 5 called.

A hand took his shoulder firmly. "Easy, there. You're going to the hospital. You've had a severe shock and—"

Jimmy Christopher, peering around, could not see Tim Donovan. "A boy was in the car," he blurted. "Where is he? He was with me when—"

"Didn't see any boy. No boy in the car when we got here. Easy, now! After a good rest in the hospital—"

Operator 5 thrust the interns aside, struggled to his feet. He knew that the sedan with the drawn blinds was gone—that the mystic in the scarlet robe had vanished with it. In Jimmy Christopher's ringing ears the pronouncement of doom echoed again: "Kasma strikes!" He heard once more the ominous rumbling, the violent crashing of a great church spilling in fragments to the ground.

"Tim!"

There could be no answer from the Irish lad, for he was not there. So clearly that Operator 5 could never forget it, he heard again the mocking laughter that had thundered out of empty space—the laughter of Kasma the Destroyer...!

CHAPTER 3
POWER OF THE AGES

THE SCREAMING of sirens shrilled over Manhattan as ponderous red fire-engines sped to the site of the wrecked church on the Drive. Cordons of police rushed in radio cars to restrain the awed crowd that gathered to see the appalling destruction. Roaring newspaper presses poured out extra editions and boys trotted the streets shouting the headlines:

Church Collapses at Command of Mystic!
Fifty Killed as Church is Destroyed!
Strange Laughter Booms from Sky!
Ministers Organize to Combat Mystic Cult!

The strident voices of the newsboys echoed in the street as Operator 5 alighted from a taxi in front of a cheap hotel on the East Side, above One Hundredth Street. The cut on his forehead was plastered; his face was drawn, his eyes darkly grim. He noted groups of men and women reading the extra editions, talking in low, awed tones. They were speaking, he knew, of the power of Kasma....

Operator 5 entered the musty lobby of the hotel with brisk step. At the desk he asked for "Mr. Sept, please." The clerk answered with "Six fourteen, sir." Jimmy Christopher stepped into an elevator, and the cab carried him upward.

The man at the desk was an Intelligence agent. The attendant in the cage was another undercover operator. No one entered here who was not a member of the service. This grimy hotel was, for the time being, the New York City headquarters of the United States Intelligence.

A short month ago it had been condemned and closed. A month hence, the headquarters would be located in another hidden spot. But today, secret wires were carrying dispatches to guarded rooms above, and from the suite of the chief, orders were being flashed.

Operator 5 again exchanged pass-
words with a sentry when he stepped
from the cab. "Z-7," the undercover
agent said quietly, "is seeing the Secretary of State now." Jimmy Christopher
had known that the Secretary of State,
whose command over the Intelligence
was supreme, was coming to Manhattan. He nodded, strode along a row of
doors, and stepped into a clattering room.

Busy teletypes were clicking; men were stationed at a bank of
switchboards; others were sitting with phones clamped to their
ears, receiving wireless dispatches. This was the vital communications division of Headquarters HN. Operator 5 asked quickly
of the nervous chief-dispatcher at the desk: "Has any information been received concerning Tim Donovan?"

"None whatever."

"Please check all hospitals in the city as fast as you can. The
moment there is word from him, I want to have it."

Operator 5 turned from the room to another door. Opening
it, he stepped into a compartment as small as a closet which
contained two double-glassed and iron-barred windows. In
the space beyond, a small, yellow-faced man in trim business
suit was sitting quietly in a chair. His face was lifted; his black,
slanted eyes were gleaming with a fanatical light. He was the
Yellowese named Zarin whose capture had started Operator 5
along the strangest trail he had ever followed.

Turning to another window, he peered at a second saffron-skinned captive. This silk-clad young man of slight frame was the unknown who had been taken prisoner at the Mexican border, who had worn the strange, thick, scarlet robe. Quietly Operator 5 turned a strong latch, and stepped into the room.

THE UNKNOWN came to his feet. His black, almond eyes burned brightly in his noble face. He kept an erect, regal bearing as Jimmy Christopher approached. Of him, Operator 5 asked quietly:

"Who are you?"

There was no answer.

"I am your friend," Jimmy Christopher said softly. "You must trust me. You must remember your high caste, the honorable memory of your ancestors. Your worship of them must not die under the power of Kasma."

At the mention of the mystic name, the gleam of the black eyes grew stronger; but the Yellowese did not speak.

"This force that has come into your mind—you must fight it. You are strong, and your own strength must save you. You must not become lost to the faith of your fathers. My friend—who are you?"

Silence. Yet, now, a dullness came into the Unknown's eyes, as though he were wondering—wondering who he was. The confusion that clouded his face told Operator 5 that this man did not know his own identity. He leaned forward and whispered urgently.

"Try to remember! Try to remember who you are! Never stop trying to remember!"

The bewilderment in the almond eyes persisted as Operator 5

quietly stepped from the room. Two Intelligence men, assigned to guard the prisoners, had entered the cubicle outside the cells. One of them remarked wearily:

"We've worn ourselves out trying to get these men to talk, but it's hopeless. They simply won't speak. Whatever this thing is they believe in, they're convinced it's all-powerful. They're afraid of nothing. A belief as strong as theirs—it kind of gets you."

"That belief," Operator 5 declared cryptically as he stepped out, "has already made hundreds of thousands of slaves in the United States."

He walked briskly, eyes darkening, into the office adjoining that of Z-7. A desk was littered with yellow flimsies, reports brought for the attention of the chief from the communication-room. Operator 5 shuffled through them quickly, and as he snatched sentences here and there, his lips pressed hard.

... HN-NY... TWO BEST OPERATORS MISSING... REASON UNKNOWN... HUNT UNDER WAY... CI (Chicago)

And:

... HN-NY... K-2 TODAY SUFFERED MENTAL COLLAPSE... CONFINED IN STATE HOSPITAL FOR INSANE... CIRCUMSTANCES BEING INVES-TIGATED... LAC (Los Angeles)

And:

... HN-NY... TWO AGENTS FOUND DEAD IN

STREET OUTSIDE SUB-HEADQUARTERS... NO INDICATIONS OF VIOLENCE OR TRACES OF POISON... REASON FOR DEATHS BAFFLING BUT SUSPECT MURDER... MF (Miami)

And:

... HN-NY... THIS SUB-HEADQUARTERS NOW UNDER ORDER V-4... W-6, CHIEF, HAS SUFFERED SUDDEN AMNESIA... UNABLE TO FULFILL DUTIES... RECOVERY VERY UNCERTAIN... BM (Boston)

JIMMY CHRISTOPHER'S eyes narrowed as he removed a leather case from his pocket and slipped several closely written pages of notes from it, to which a sheaf of newspaper clippings was attached. He waited, hearing voices beyond the connecting door—one sharp and curt, that of the Secretary of State, the other throaty and low, that of the Washington chief of the Intelligence, Z-7. The sudden opening of another door, giving off the communications division, startled Operator 5.

The chief-dispatcher hurried in, thrust a flimsy toward Jimmy Christopher, and exclaimed: "Great God—read that!"

The message, just off the teletype wires, widened Operator 5's eyes:

... HN-NY... REPORTING COMPLETE DESTRUCTION CHURCH OF THE HOLY MOTHER... GREAT STRUCTURE COLLAPSED SOON AFTER NEWS OF NEW YORK TRAGEDY AND IN MIDST OF SERVICE...

MYSTIC IN RED ROBE APPEARED DECLARING
HIMSELF SON OF KASMA... MYSTIC ESCAPED IN
TERRORIZED CROWD... AS CHURCH FELL THUN-
DERCLAP SOUNDED LIKE GLOATING LAUGH-
TER... CITY HORRIFIED... FEAR AND WORSHIP
OF KASMA BECOMING WIDESPREAD... INVES-
TIGATION GETTING NO RESULTS... AWAITING
ORDERS... PHP (Philadelphia)

Operator 5 held the dispatch in a cold hand as he strode to
the door of Z-7's inner office. He thrust his way in, and the two
men turned to face him. The ebon eyes of the Washington chief
widened with surprise at the interruption; the high, stern forehead of the Secretary of State furrowed angrily. Jimmy Christopher extended the message and exclaimed:

"I interrupt only because this is extremely urgent. Somehow,
and at once, we must organize to combat this strange power of
Kasma. Unless we do, this mystic faith will sweep across the
United States and command all the people!"

The Secretary scowled as he read the message. He listened
with growing impatience as Jimmy Christopher rapidly told of
the utter havoc striking the great Church of the Divine. Z-7's
eyes glittered blackly as the story unfolded, and profound mystification shone in them. When Operator 5 paused, the Secretary
peered at him contemptuously.

"You expect me to believe that?"

"It is exactly what happened, sir. I was an eye-witness. I have
stated only facts."

The Secretary uttered a scoffing laugh. "You expect me to

believe that this mysterious man in the red robe called upon his god to destroy a Christian church, and that church was immediately destroyed?"

"Precisely, sir!"

"You declare that the instant the church crumbled to the ground, a great thunderclap sounded, though the sky was perfectly clear and there was no storm—a burst of thunder which you say was laughter."

"It was, sir, without a doubt, laughter that seemed to come out of cosmic space."

"Nonsense!" the Secretary snorted. "The thing is impossible! I put no stock in it."

GRIMLY OPERATOR 5 declared: "You cannot doubt, sir, that two churches have been completely wrecked by some strange force. Do you think it was purely accidental that both crumbled to bits in the midst of their services? Can you believe that the man in the red robe, who calls himself the Son of Kasma, had nothing whatever to do with it?"

"Whatever has happened," the Secretary of State declared frostily, "it is a matter outside the field of the Intelligence Service."

"Sir," Operator 5 bent tensely across the desk, "nothing that affects the welfare of the nation is outside the field of the Intelligence Service. Kasma is a threat upon the very existence of the United States. Picture, sir, if you can, the result when the spread of the cult of Kasma reaches from coast to coast. The fear and worship of a hundred million people will make the Son of Kasma all powerful!"

"It is still my opinion that the matter is outside—"

"When operators in our Intelligence Service are murdered apparently without a cause, when our undercover agents are strangely stricken with loss of memory, when man after man of them go stark, raving mad—that situation, sir, becomes a vital matter to the Service because, if it continues, it will wipe the Intelligence out of existence."

The Secretary stared. "Have you too gone mad?" he demanded. "You're talking like an insane person."

"I assure you there is a connection, sir," Jimmy Christopher hurried on. "A direct connection between the destruction of the churches, the crippling of our service, and the strange cloud-bursts which have occurred at scattered points. The same power—the force of Kasma, whatever it might be—is the cause of all these things."

The Secretary turned stiffly. "Z-7, I have no time to listen to this young man's ranting. If you put any stock in what he says, listen to him. All I will say now is that unless he brings me abso-

JIMMY CHRISTOPHER

lute proof of his wild statements, the Intelligence Service must keep hands off.

"You already have standing orders, young man," the Secretary declared, turning to Operator 5, "to run down the leader of the organization known as the Hidden Hundred.* So far you have failed to unmask him."

Operator 5 straightened coldly, his eyes glittering.

"We know," the Secretary snapped, "that the members of the Hidden Hundred are all ex-Intelligence men. They have built themselves into a subversive organization, under the pretext of serving their country, and they must be destroyed. We have agreed that the way to destroy them is to capture their leader. That is a task which you must consider paramount, Operator 5. Your job now is to run that man to earth—and therefore I further order you to abandon this fantastic case of the destroying god."

"Good Lord, sir!" Operator 5 blurted. "Do you mean that you will allow us to do nothing—while our best operators are being murdered, their memories destroyed, driven mad by—"

"Proof," the Secretary interrupted. "I demand it before you make a single move. Operator 5, listen to me. I am a hard-shelled, matter-of-fact man. I was brought up strictly in the Christian belief. I do not hesitate to say that the immorality of this war-breeding, sin-spreading world of today leads me to conclude that Christianity has failed. If, then, this deity called Kasma possesses the power you say, I for one am almost willing to embrace his faith in the hope that it will lead civilization away from otherwise inevitable destruction."

OPERATOR 5 gazed appalled after the Secretary as the door

---

* AUTHOR's NOTE: The Hidden Hundred first appeared in the Operator 5 narrative entitled "Legions of the Death Master."

slammed. Z-7, stunned at the amazing statement, gazed deep into Jimmy Christopher's eyes. There was silence until Operator 5 said in a hushed tone:

"That—that attitude—is exactly why hundreds of thousands of American men and women are turning their backs on Christianity and worshiping Kasma at this very hour!"

Z-7 spoke quietly. "Operator 5, there's no operator in the Intelligence who had given greater service to his country than you have. There's no agent I think more highly of than you. Time and again, you've risked your life on dangerous cases—over and over you've unearthed intrigues that might have destroyed us all, and every time you defeated them. When you report, I consider your every word important. Yet now, even I am skeptical of what you say."

Operator 5 promptly spread his notes and the newspaper clippings on the desk. Quickly he pointed to one after another, as he rapidly explained them.

"Here, Chief, are newspaper accounts of mysterious falls of rain in the Middle-Western region which is stricken by the dust storms. For years, nature has been slowly turning that vast area into a desert. Today, countless farms are buried under thick dust and sand. The drought more than a year ago was only the beginning of a national disaster which has brought hundreds of thousands face to face with utter despair and hopelessness. Can you blame those stricken people if they turn to follow the mystic belief of a man who can cause rain to fall in the desert at the lift of a hand, at the speaking of a single command?"

Operator 5 indicated the clippings which told of the scattered downpours that had occurred following the operations of mysterious rain-makers. In the havoc-spread section suffocated by repeated dust storms, rain had miraculously fallen at scattered points—not mere showers, but veritable torrents which had changed the dry earth into rich soil. And in each case, rumor associated a red-robed man with the strange phenomenon. These crimson-cloaked figures had appeared, had gathered the stricken farmer families around them, had commanded rain to fall—and the skies had instantly yielded water!

"Three nights ago I saw it happen, Chief—a downpour in the center of the desert, at the height of the dry season. It was used as a cover under which a small army of aliens were smuggled into the United States. Those aliens spread the cult of Kasma. Hordes of them have already found their way into the country.

"On these other occasions, the rain-making phenomenon was used to display, to these stricken people, the power of Kasma—to recruit them to the mystic faith. Chief, today, on this very Sunday, the Christian churches in that region are empty while literally hundreds of thousands worship Kasma as the true god."

Z-7 stared.

"Now the weapon of Kasma is terror! At a mere word from the Son of Kasma, Christian churches crash to the ground. Before the very eyes of hundreds of Christians today this power—a force out of cosmic space, from which the name of Kasma is derived—struck. They saw Kasma break down the houses of their own God, destroying unbelievers. There can be only one result. These people, panic-stricken, will flock to the faith of Kasma in frantic self-preservation."

"You cannot believe that the Son of Kasma actually wields such a weapon!" Z-7 protested.

"He does, Chief. Twice I've seen it work its wonders. Twice I've heard the mocking laughter of Kasma come out of the empty sky. I have felt that power myself—the same force that is destroying the Intelligence Service, because our Service is the greatest enemy the cult of Kasma faces."

The door opened quickly; the chief-dispatcher put three yellow flimsies into the hand of Z-7, and withdrew. The Washington chief was too absorbed in the amazing statements of Operator 5 to glance at them.

"That force struck me in the air when I was flying above the border. It filled me with a strange hysteria. I might have gone mad, like Border Patrolman Hunter, if I hadn't somehow managed to fly away from it. I felt that same force again this morning when I was following the Son of Kasma's car. I saw C-6 go mad before my eyes. Again, we might all have become raving maniacs if the effect hadn't resulted in C-6's losing control of the car—the wreck.

"I am absolutely convinced, Chief, that in every case it's the same power—a power that can bring rain, destroy great buildings, make men mad, or kill them instantly without leaving a trace."

Z-7 BENT across the desk intently. "You do not believe this is a supernatural power. I know you too well for that. But if it isn't—what the devil is it?"

Operator 5 explained quickly how he had stationed four men around the Church of the Divine in an attempt to learn

TIM DONOVAN

the nature of the force. He repeated his orders and their reports. Briskly he stated his conclusion:

"The power is not electrical in nature. As for what it actually is—Chief, I'm absolutely baffled. I am going to try to learn the secret by means of further tests. It may be several forces used together, and one of them—that which turns men into maniacs and instantly kills—might be an invisible gas."

Z-7 was peering strangely at Operator 5. "God!" he exclaimed. "What can we do?"

"Whatever we do, chief, we *must* combat the cult of Kasma with all our resources—or this nation is doomed!"

Again the door opened and the chief-dispatcher stepped in quickly. His trembling fingers held a saffron flimsy which he thrust at Z-7. He blurted: "This has just come over the air, without distorter. It's not one of our codes. I can't make head or tail of it."

Jimmy Christopher, at a glance, exclaimed: "That's from Tim Donovan! It's a special cipher we use between us. Let me read that!"

Quickly he translated the cryptic symbols of the message. The system was one by which one or two letters became a word, a method of telegraphic shorthand for use when lack of time

was an emergency. The meaningless letters became, in Operator 5's mind:

NOT HURT IN WRECK—TRAILED CAR—TAKEN
PRISONER TRYING TO GET INTO BUILDING—
HUGE TEMPLE—MANAGED TO BREAK REACH
RADIO TRANSMITTER—WILL BE FOUND SOON—
MAN IN RED ROBE HERE—ADDRESS—

There, at its most vital point, the message ended! Operator 5's lips pressed hard as he faced Z-7. "Tim's a prisoner—and he didn't get a chance to say where he is being held! They found him sending the message. He's located a temple of Kasma in this city. Chief, we've got to—"

The chief-dispatcher had left the room hurriedly; and now he again rushed in. As he passed four reports to Z-7 he exclaimed: "Exactly like the first three, chief! What the devil is happening?"

Z-7 had been too profoundly interested in Operator 5's report to read the first three messages. Now he glanced over seven, startlingly alike in their information. He rose tensely from his desk and his ebon eyes glittered.

"Great Scott! Seven kidnappings reported through the Department of Justice*—all occurring within the last few

---

* AUTHOR'S NOTE: The Bureau of Investigation of the Department of Justice (which must be differentiated in the reader's mind from the U.S. Intelligence and many other investigating branches of the federal government) is fighting a relentless war against crime, and particularly kidnapping. At a telephone in the Bureau in Washington, a special agent is on constant duty.

hours—and all of them Christian church men! Seven ministers vanished in New York! In God's name, this devil's brew is—"

"We've got to find the Temple of Kasma, chief!" Operator 5 declared ringingly. "We've got to throw all our men into the field and somehow—"

"We can't move without the consent of the Secretary of State!" Z-7 snapped. "You know his strict orders. Unless he authorizes me to go ahead, I can't—" The chief broke off, swinging wide the door of the clattering communications-room. "Locate the Secretary! As soon as possible."

Operator 5 demanded sharply: "You mean you will do nothing unless the Secretary consents?"

"I am bound by his orders. I can do nothing else."

Jimmy Christopher's eyes darkened. "Chief, Tim is in danger. I'm going to find him, and I'm not going to wait for permission. If the Secretary decides to break me for insubordination—all right!"

He opened the entrance of Z-7's inner office, paused, peering back, a swift plan forming in his mind.

"I ask your permission on one point, though, Chief. I took the Yellowese, Zarin, prisoner. Now I ask that he be placed in

That instrument can be reached from any telephone in the country, for the purpose of reporting a kidnapping, by calling a special number. Within ten minutes the Director of the Bureau will be notified and special agents dispatched to the scene of the crime, by plane if necessary. It is well to know this number that is an aid of the government in its constant fight against abduction. It is National 7117.

my custody. Don't refuse, Chief! It's my only hope of reaching Tim—a long gamble—but my only hope… Chief?"

"You have my permission," Z-7 answered, "but you must answer to the Secretary for disregarding his orders."

Operator 5 snapped the door shut, strode swiftly to the cell in which a mute disciple of a mystic god was being held captive—his first desperate move in a quickly formulated plan to reach the Hidden Temple of Kasma….

CHAPTER 4
THE FINGER OF DEATH

A LEERING face looked out of the entrance of a small building on Walnut Street, in Kansas City; white-rimmed eyes peered at the crowds on the sidewalk, at the stream of cars in the street. Patrolman Michael Horrigan, directing traffic on the corner, did not notice. It was not until a woman screamed wildly, not until he glimpsed a furtive man lurking there in the entrance of the building, that he looked into those mad eyes.

Pedestrians were hurrying past the building, startled by the scream of the woman who had seen the crouching man's frightful face, when Patrolman Horrigan approached. He scowled at the man with the wild eyes. The white-circled pupils glared. The huddled figure swayed like a gorilla. A snarl broke from this man's bared teeth as Horrigan spoke:

"Come out of there! What's the matter with you? You better come along with me and—"

The man in the doorway leaped. Horrigan stumbled backward, blinded by the scraping of sharp fingernails across his eyes. He gasped with pain, blinked through stinging blood to see his assailant whirling away, darting on bent legs, arms swinging like a prowling ape's. He saw the man's hand drag an automatic from an armpit holster. Suddenly shots rang out and bullets screamed as they caromed off building fronts.

Women shrieked and ran; men darted for cover; children fled frantically. Again and again the automatic barked as the crouching man deliberately turned it upon terrorized pedestrians seeking shelter in doorways. Horrigan sprinted forward with a gasp of dismay. "Drop that gun!" he roared. "Drop it!" And the black muzzle of the automatic turned upon him.

A savage snarl from the lips of the crouching man followed the next blasting shot. Horrigan staggered, with pain burning his arm where the bullet drilled through. His service gat blazed twice, swiftly. A shrieking cry broke from the man with the automatic as he lurched forward. For a full minute, he groveled on the pavement, howling, gibbering, tearing at his clothing, while red froth bubbled on his lips. A horrible convulsion shook him before death sprawled him lax in the Sunday sun.

Horrigan made haste to put his report through the nearest call-box. He ordered the collecting crowd back. He shoved at a young man who said he was a newspaper reporter, who followed one quick question with another. He blurted:

"He started shootin', that's all. He was crazy! I'm sorry I had to do it, but there wasn't any other way. Stark, starin' mad, I tell you! No, I don't know who he is."

One man in the collecting crowd might have told Patrolman Horrigan who the dead man was. He turned away—a wiry figure with white hair, his eyes grim, shadowed under lowered brows. He was one designated in the United States Intelligence Service as M-8; he was chief of sub-headquarters KCM. He knew that the man who lay dead on the pavement was D-3, one of his best agents. Keen witted, level-headed, reliable in his shrewd judgments—M-8 remembered D-3 as that kind of a man.

Yet now he lay dead on the pavement while a bewildered patrolman muttered to a reporter: "Crazy, he was—stark, killin' crazy…!"

IN SAN FRANCISCO, Operator H-4 of the United States Intelligence walked slowly along a musty street leading toward the famed Embarcadero. He appeared to be merely strolling, sightseeing; but his keen eyes glanced again and again at a sandaled Yellowese shuffling into the Chinatown district.

H-4 was acting upon special orders received at SFC from WDC-13, the central office of the Intelligence—orders which read: "Watch all Orientals suspected of recent illegal entry." H-4 was certain he had spotted a new face, a man who had been recently smuggled into the country. He was prepared to follow the suspect until he could report this as a certainty.

He was destined never to complete his detail, never to make his report. Suddenly he dropped....

He lay still on the pavement, surrounded by water-front toughs and Orientals with inscrutable faces until an ambulance approached with clanging bell. Two white-uniformed men stepped from it with a litter. They bent over H-4; they made an examination; they peered at each other puzzledly.

"Dead," one said. "Dead as a doornail. But what killed him? There's not the slightest sign...."

THE SHRILL blast of a police whistle riffled above the hum of the heavy Sunday traffic on Queensboro Bridge, New York City. Drivers' feet slapped to their brake-pedals. Bumpers clinked as car jolted against car. Engines idled as an angry traffic officer strode to the center of the span, toward a man who was wandering directly across the traffic lanes.

"Where do you think you're goin'?" he bawled. "Tryin' to get run over? You can't pile 'em up on me! You're goin' to the station for this! What's your name?"

The man who had caused the abrupt stop of the crowded automobiles was garbed in dark clothing; he was wearing a clergyman's stock. He looked around as if in a dream and mumbled: "I—I don't know, officer!"

"What? You tryin' to tell me you don't know who you are?"

"Of course, I—I have a name, but—I can't remember it. I've been trying. I—I can't recall how I got here. There's something wrong with my mind, I'm afraid. I'm trying to find something I might recognize, but everything—all this is so strange...."

The patrolman stared. He grasped the clergyman's arm. Traffic resumed its swift flow over the bridge, and finally a radio patrol car drew up. It carried the dark-frocked man away. When the two puzzled squad-car men took their charge into the precinct station, the desk sergeant stared in dismay while he heard the story.

"Take him into the Inspector's office. I'm calling a doctor. I've seen that man's picture in the papers plenty of times. He's Bishop Danley. One of the greatest religious leaders in the city, that man!... Strange—can't remember who he is...."

FROM ONE of the great piers on the opposite side of the island of Manhattan, a trans-Atlantic steamer had put out the previous evening. Its churning screws had driven it far into the open ocean. Among its passengers were hundreds of members of the clergy on their way to Geneva to assemble with colleagues from all over the world in the yearly Congress of Christian Faiths. While the *Bethlehem* plowed through a smooth, calm sea, they gathered this afternoon in the quiet salon of the steamer for worship.

Captain Eric Janssen was standing straddled on the bridge, peering over water smooth as a mirror, when his First Officer hurried to his side. No word passed between them for a moment. They peered around in bewilderment. They were as accustomed to the vibration of the *Bethlehem's* engines as to the beating of their own hearts; but the tremor that was passing through the great ship now was new to them—startling!

"You feel it too, sir!" the First Officer exclaimed. "I felt in on deck. It's getting stronger all the time. Some thing's shaking the ship. What the devil—?"

The vibration grew stronger even as the words were spoken. The bridge trembled under the feet of the two officers. Their ruddy cheeks jiggled. Swiftly it became so violent that it blurred their eyesight, made them grasp a handrail for support. They peered down on the deck, saw bewildered men and women hurrying from the cabins. Fright—outright fear—was pictured on the faces of the passengers as the great ship quaked with a power that threatened to tear her seams asunder.

"In God's name, Captain, what is it?"

Captain Janssen's hand shot to the engine-room telegraph. His signal tinkled far below the water-line, and instantly the Chief Engineer relayed it to the crew. He had hurried to his post in alarm, thinking that something was wrong with the power-plant He had found the engines functioning smoothly; but now the captain's command stopped them. Steam sizzled as the pistons sighed to a standstill and the gigantic propeller shafts ceased turning. But still—more violently every moment—the terrific vibration shook the great ship.

On deck, hundreds of passengers milled, eyes shining with terror. The quaking of the deck beneath their feet was so strong that they could not stand unsupported. They clung to the rails, peering around in abject bewilderment and consternation. All about the *Bethlehem,* the sea was glassy smooth. The great ship plowed ahead without power and her movement created the only breath of wind upon that water. The sun beamed out of a sky obscured by only a single white cloud. Yet, in the midst of that perfect tranquility, the huge vessel was tearing herself to pieces!

A frantic voice on the ship's telephone carried a hysterical message to the bridge.

"The seams are opening! The plates are cracking! The ship's breaking apart!"

Captain Janssen's trembling hand touched a switch; instantly, from stem to stern of the vessel, alarm gongs clanged. "Take to the boats!" that meant. Up the companionways the crew came scrambling madly, whipped into action by the barking commands of frantic officers. Davits creaked as the first of the life-boats began to swing from its trestles; yet the men who operated the winches could scarcely stand erect due to the wrenching of the ship.

"All passengers to the boats!"

Now the sea was billowing, waves were rolling—created by the ship itself as it rocked! An ominous roaring from below warned the desperate officers that water was pouring through the cracking hull. As it shook and rolled, as the power of the violent vibrations became even greater, the ship listed heavily. The lifeboats were still swinging above the rocking water when a deafening, ripping shock struck the steamer.

THE *BETHLEHEM* literally was cleaved to pieces. It split and burst as the screams of the doomed mixed with the hissing of liberated, scalding steam—screams that were stifled instantly by the waves which washed her tilting decks. So swiftly that few had time to leap across the vibrating rails, the majestic steamer foundered. A few moments before the vessel had been steaming serenely on its lane; now, in one cataclysmic moment, it became disintegrating wreckage plunging to the ocean's bed!

Lashing waves churned as the *Bethlehem* vanished. Men and women thrown into the water struggled frantically to escape the voracious whirlpool created by the sinking ship. They grasped at splintered debris desperately. They peered stunned across a sea rolling with scattered wreckage on which there was no other ship in sight.

And they heard a deafening clap of thunder roll out of the sky—a booming burst that roared out of space and echoed back into the vastness from which it came. They heard the mockery of a destructive god as death faced them—the gloating laughter of Kasma!...

An SOS, flashing across the six-hundred-meter wave-band of the wireless spectrum, silenced every broadcasting station in the East. The whine of a dot-dash message carried through the ether and brought the news of a frightful disaster to land. Dispatches flashed over the electrical webs of the great news services and newspaper presses roared. Newsboys raced the special editions into the streets:

Bethlehem Sinks; Only 20 Survivors!
Rescued Declare Strange Power Sank Ship: Hundreds of
Religious Leaders Lost!
Mocking Laughter Heard as Ship Plunges!
Only Surviving Clergyman, Hysterical, Declares Breth-
ren Destroyed by Wrath of Mystic Deity Kasma!

The cries of the newsboys loping through the streets did not reach into a certain room that was utterly black, utterly silent.

It might have been empty, its quiet was so complete—but in the utter darkness there were presences.

A faint gleam appeared within the dark-draped walls. It grew slowly brighter, shining upon a grotesque figure. The being who appeared out of the gloom seemed to be a clothed skeleton—a creature of dry bones, who lived!

The head of this apparition was a fleshless skull, but live, sharp eyes shone in the bony sockets of the head. Its hands were claws of bare bone. As the shine of the light increased, it shone upon a score of other similar, living skeletons in the room.

They stood silent a moment, men whose heads were covered with black masks painted white to simulate the face of Death. Their hands were covered with gloves painted to look like fleshless fingers. They were part of a secret organization known as the Hidden Hundred; the masked man who faced them was their captain!

These strange masks covered the faces of men who had formerly been members of the United States Intelligence. They had served their country in its most vital defense organization; they had given their strength and brains and lives in full devotion. They had faced death recklessly in urgent cases upon which the welfare of their nation depended. Yet a single act of one man had cast them out....

THE SECRETARY OF STATE, taking charge of the Intelligence over Z-7, had, because of dangerous international situations, forced inaction on the Service through fear of precipitating a crisis that might lead to war. Untrained in the ways of the Service, occupied first with the trying duties of the State

Department, the Secretary had ordered new regulations into effect which further hampered the activities of the system. Because the Intelligence found itself faced with gigantic tasks while gravely undermanned, the Hidden Hundred had sprung into existence.

Their leader had recruited them into the outlaw organization; had bound them with vows of allegiance, had covered their operations with secrecy. The Hidden Hundred served the country which had renounced them—which was seeking to make them pay for their loyalty with their lives!

Into the silence of this hidden headquarters, the voice of the leader of the Hidden Hundred came softly:

"Comrades, we face a crisis. We take up today the fight against the power of Kasma. Every moment is precious. Listen well!"

The skeletons' live eyes did not waver from those of the leader.

"In spite of the grave danger from our brothers of the Intelligence, we must fight against Kasma—or else we shall see our government crumble, our wealth confiscated, our people enslaved by a devil's power that mercilessly destroys.

"In this city stands a temple erected to Kasma. It is well hidden. Now, for the first time, the location of that temple has become known to one outside the mystic circle of Kasma. Within its walls are secrets which we must learn if we are to crush this evil force. Comrades—will you follow me into the Temple of Kasma!"

A chorus rose from the living death's-heads. "We will follow!"

"Then listen! Operator 5, of the Intelligence, by a subterfuge, has learned the location of the temple. He had captured one called Zarin. Today he arranged that this Yellowese might escape headquarters HN. Zarin, not knowing his escape was planned, stole from his cell to another room and, by means of a fire escape, got out of the building. Operator 5 trailed him. The fanatical follower of the cult of Kasma unwittingly led him to the hidden temple. He cannot hope to penetrate it alone. We must assist him. Orders!"

The hushed voice continued to speak rapidly. The bony forefinger of the captain indicated one member of the Hidden Hundred after another as he explained each detail of his strategy for entering the house of mystic worship. Once his plan was completely outlined, he paused, searching the eyes of the men whose heads were fleshless skulls.

"Follow instructions—now!"

The single light in the room dimmed. A faint rustle sounded as draperies swung. The leader of the secret organization had withdrawn.

He walked quickly along a black hallway into a small black room which served as his operations-office. He heard a step, looked up to see another skull-headed figure approaching him. The member of the Hidden Hundred known as X-13 spoke quickly, his voice anxious.

"Captain—you know what your appearing again may mean. Not only danger from the followers of Kasma, but capture by the Intelligence. Let me lead these men. Don't expose yourself to this danger!"

The hunted leader answered quietly: "Conduct the men to their objective, X-13. I will follow at once."

He closed the door. In a dim, gray glow, he pulled the black gloves from his hands. He loosened the weird mask, and took it from his head. He stuffed the disguise into an inner pocket; and his blue eyes gleamed darkly in the light. He was Operator 5!

A HEAVY truck rumbled along a side street in the smart residential district flanking the East River, in the Fifties, on Manhattan. Here, new apartment buildings reared at the very edge of the murky water, their high windows overlooking the giant bridges and the hooting river traffic. The truck snarled up the ramp of a garage located directly across the broad street from one of the towers.

Operator 5 was at the wheel. Quietly he explained to the anxious, mild-mannered man sitting beside him: "I saw Zarin's taxi go into this garage. When it came out a few moments later, it was empty. I came in on a pretext and saw no sign of him. Next, I watched outside, and I saw an unknown Yellowese enter the apartment building opposite."

"You're sure there's a connection between the two places?"

"There must be, Dad."

John Christopher had once been Operator Q-6 in the United States Intelligence. A serious gunshot wound had forced him from the service, obliged him to lead a life of inactivity. Two bullets lay so close to his heart that no surgeon dared remove them, yet they constantly threatened him with sudden death. Wearied of inaction, Operator 5's father had become a member of the Hidden Hundred under his son. He had accepted the code name of a man who had died in the service of the secret order—X-13.

Nerves tense, eyes sharp, Operator 5 sent the truck crawl-ing into the gloomy, chill interior of the cavernous garage. As he brought it to a stop, two men with ominous, ugly faces approached from a partitioned office. Bulges beneath their coats revealed that they were well armed. One of them declared harshly: "Got no room for you here, buddy. We're full up."

Operator 5 declared tightly: "We're staying anyway!"

As he spoke, the heavy tail-gate of the truck slammed down. Weird figures leaped from the truck. Beings with skeleton heads and skeletal hands, leveling automatics. Their appearance was so sudden, so startling, that the two garage men were paralyzed with bewilderment. As a full score of members of the Hidden Hundred began scattering through the garage, one of the two wheeled in consternation, raced toward the office.

Operator 5 sped after him. He slapped through the narrow door and snatched up a telephone. His one hand lifted the receiver; his other whipped out an automatic as Jimmy Chris-topher delivered a swift, stiff-fingered blow to his neck. It sent a chill shock through him and staggered him. Operator 5 snatched the telephone from his grimy hands and followed as a single rocking report cracked from the automatic….

The bullet tugged at Jimmy Christopher's sleeve. His stiff fingers again sent a sharp, twisting blow to the neck of the man with the gun. A thick finger was squeezing the trigger of the automatic when the paralytic effect took hold. Instantly, the garage man stiffened. There was a sharp, noiseless intake of breath as he sagged against the wall, rigid as a statue. Operator

5 stood poised, hearing the sounds of swift, concerted movement in the garage.

He had seized the telephone before the receiver could be lifted. Now he lowered it quickly, gripped the arms of the unconscious man. The paralyzing jiu-jitsu blow would keep that man unconscious, Operator 5 knew, for about an hour. He lowered the garage man to the floor, took the automatic, jerked the telephone cords from the wall-box, stepped out and turned the key in the lock.

The members of the Hidden Hundred had acted swiftly, according to plan. Some of them had surrounded the second garage man. Held powerless, his wrists and ankles were being bound with sticky tire-tape. As a gag was held ready to be thrust into his mouth, Jimmy Christopher strode to him quickly. His voice rang with determination as he demanded:

"Where is the entrance to the temple of Kasma?"

THE PRISONER'S eyes lighted with consternation; but he did not speak. Operator 5 wasted no time questioning him further. At his signal, the members of the Hidden Hundred gagged the captive, carried him to a sedan in the garage and left him inside it. Another squad of the skeleton-headed men had closed the outer doors and fastened them. Only a few yellow bulbs lighted the chill space as the living skeletons gathered around Operator 5.

"In a few minutes," he explained, "our second squad, unmasked, will attempt to get into the apartment house through the public entrance. We've got to get inside as quickly as they do. Look for a passage leading under the street. Move fast!"

As the spectral figures scattered in search, Jimmy Christopher hurried toward a ramp which led to a vast storage-space below the street level. Ex-Operator Q-6 kept at his side as they strode along lines of cars. The walls were of whitewashed brick; there seemed to be no place where a tunnel entrance might be hidden; but Operator 5's sharp eyes searched out every possibility.

"The devil only knows what may have happened to Tim by now, Dad!" he exclaimed anxiously. "We've got to find the way that—"

He paused, gazing at a huge truck which was backed to the wall. He peered into the narrow crack which separated its rear end and the whitewashed bricks; then he climbed quickly to the seat. Unlatching a narrow door behind the driver's compartment, he peered into the black hollow of the truck body, and felt a cold draft flow past him. Immediately he exclaimed: "It's here!" and a low whistle came from his lips.

Operator 5 gestured his father after him as he crawled into the black space. The skull-headed members of the Hidden Hundred, answering the signal whistle, hurried down the ramp and followed, Jimmy Christopher found that a section of the wall had been ripped out. The truck, backed so closely to it, concealed the opening. He crawled through, listened, waited breathlessly while the Hidden Hundred groped after him.

"Watch sharp!" he urged in a whisper. "It's impossible to know what we may run into. You understand as well as I how deadly the power of Kasma is—a power to kill, to destroy the mind. Keep together—and remember, more than anything else, that we want to capture the Son of Kasma if it is possible."

Jimmy Christopher had brought a small electric torch from his pocket. Now he touched the contact and a pencil-thin beam shot along a cement-walled passage that dipped downward. He began following it, the skull-headed members of his hunted band behind him. They knew that the tunnel passed beneath the street; its direction confirmed Operator 5's surmise that it connected with the suspected apartment house. Now the floor sloped upward from its lowest point, and the slender line of Operator 5's light played upon a blank wall. With the Hidden Hundred behind him, he stopped at the point where the passage came to a dead end.

Completely baffled for a moment, he studied the cement wall and the pattern of criss-cross marks on it. His keen eyes detected a concealed series of cracks forming the outline of a secret door. There was no knob, no keyhole, no apparent means of opening it. Jimmy Christopher shouldered against it, but it was immovable. He peered around, and his eyes lighted when they turned upon two bolt heads in the side wall.

APPARENTLY THESE two studs were part of the reinforcement of the walls. Operator 5 raised his automatic and with it touched both at the same time. Immediately a faint rumbling sound followed. His heart speeded when he realized that he had luckily discovered the secret of the hidden door. The metal of his gun had completed an electrical circuit between the two studs. Slowly, ponderously, the cement slab swung outward while the skeleton-headed men peered in astonishment.

When the door stopped, a single bulb flashed on in the space beyond. Its gleam illumined a steel-walled cell—the cab of a secret elevator. Quietly Operator 5 stepped into it, his men following. Only two buttons were on the small panel on one side of the cage. Jimmy Christopher touched the upper. Immediately, machinery rumbled again; the heavy slab swung shut; and with a slow, gliding movement the steel box began to rise.

There was no sound save the tense breathing of the men in the cab, the faint whining of a cable as the cage rose. Operator 5 watched a flat cement wall passing downward. For long minutes the cage climbed, the wall moved—lifting Operator 5 and his men toward unknown danger. The steel box was still rising slowly when faint sounds reached it—sounds scarcely audible, but startling!

Sharp, ringing reports, like the cracking of guns. Hoarse cries of alarm. Guttural tones shouting sudden commands. More slapping reports—and then silence.

The cage glided upward slowly.

"We must be just passing the lower floor!" Operator 5 whispered. "Perhaps it means our second squad has been stopped!"

70

THE SON of KASMA

Every man in the cage realized that if this was true, the danger confronting them was many times increased, yet none of them spoke. They held their automatics ready, waited while the wall in front of them dropped downward at its slow, agonizing rate.

Operator 5 took his skull mask and claw gloves from his pocket as the box mounted, and drew them on. John Christopher followed his example. During the interval while the cab slowly climbed, its prisoners were silent—an uncanny group of beings whose heads were skulls in which live eyes gleamed.

Then—a clacking sound, a faint bound of the car on its cable. The wall ceased moving. In front of the cage now was another criss-crossed pattern of lines. Automatically machinery whirred again. With torturous slowness another cement slab began to swing open. Operator 5 and his men of the Hidden Hundred poised tensely as it yielded upon a dimly lighted cavity beyond.

Immediately the space was wide enough, Jimmy Christopher shouldered through. He sprang aside, facing a small room that was amber-lighted. As he stood motionless, a heavy pair of crimson drapes at the far side rustled and parted. Two Yellowese in black robes stepped inward—stopped, consternation blazing in their black, slanted eyes.

Instantly, they whirled to escape. Operator 5 sprang toward them, realizing their intent to warn others beyond. He gripped the black-sleeved arm of one of the pair, whirled that man back. His automatic poked hard against the body of the second. Immediately the members of the Hidden Hundred, rushing through the yielding secret door, crowded around the black-robed pair. The claw hands of the skeletons clamped hard across the mouths of the Yellowese.

Operator 5 stepped toward them swiftly. His hands darted to the thin yellow throats of the two captives. With swift dexterity, he pressed his thumbs on vital nerve-centers. A sharp intake of breath came from each man; a quick rigidity seized the lean bodies. The Hidden Hundred carried the two black-robed men back, left them lying rigid in the secret elevator.

They paused in the draped room. The air was oily with heady incense. A strange tension played through the air, hinting of presences beyond. Through the thick, scarlet curtains, a weird series of sounds played!—the vibrate tones of note-less, rhythm-less music. Out of the spaces beyond the curtains, the uncanny tones carried, weaving an exotic spell which brought a chill to the masked members of the Hidden Hundred, which filled Operator 5 with dread.

They stood, now, at the very portals of the hidden Temple of Kasma...!

CHAPTER 5
DELUGE OF DOOM

THE AIR sang with the uncanny melody that issued from the depths of the secret temple as Operator 5's signal gathered the skeletal figures close around him.

He whispered: "We do not know how many are here. We do not know how far we can go without being discovered. We dare not separate. In case of attack, remember—make captives but shoot in order to kill to protect yourself—Kasma will not hesitate to destroy you if you falter."

His hand went quietly to the heavy scarlet drapes. He drew them aside, and found three concealed doors. He turned from the one through which the two black-cloaked Yellowese had entered, and his hand tightened on the knob of another. Finding the way barred, he brought a pack of keys from an inner pocket and deftly tried one after another.

The sixth drew the bolt. These master implements had cost Operator 5 long nights of painstaking toil in his workshop, and now they served him well. He stepped through into a gloomy hallway, and the members of the Hidden Hundred followed. With the door closed behind them, Jimmy Christopher led his men toward a series of doors from which dim light glowed.

The doors were barred. Each gave into a small room; and in each room the windows were also barred. In the bare spaces of these rooms stood listless men and women. They peered as Operator 5 paused, gazing in, his men behind him. His heart went cold as he looked upon the faces of those held prisoner in this series of cells. None of the captives spoke; the impassive expression of their faces did not change. None of them evinced the slightest surprise at seeing the group of weird skeleton-headed figures pass their barred doors.

With silent step, dismay mounting each moment, Jimmy Christopher led his cordon to the far end of the corridor. There he paused with his eyes glittering darkly through his mask.

"Great God, captain!" one of the Hidden Hundred whispered. "Those men and women—you recognized them?"

Operator 5 had seen, in that row of cells, three ministers famed throughout the nation; he had seen four members of the United States Congress; he had seen two women celebrated as social leaders among the New York elite; he had recognized two men who were members of the United States Intelligence. The bright glint of his eyes grew sharper as he observed in a bitter whisper:

"Their minds have been destroyed—every one of them has been turned into an imbecile—by the devilish power of Kasma!"

The Hidden Hundred peered bewildered at their captain as he quietly opened a door at the end of the corridor. Silently he entered another scarlet-draped room. Here the uncanny music of Kasma was more distinct in the air, weaving a hypnotic spell with its sliding cadence of tone. The music was a strange, vibrant interweaving of note through note that blended into no tune at all, but created an eerie discord which stunned the nerves and penetrated the mind. While the pitch rose and fell disturbingly, Jimmy Christopher again sought doors behind the scarlet drapes.

He sensed that the absence of priests in these recesses of the temple meant that an assembly had met somewhere beyond—that something of strange import was occurring in the center of this edifice dedicated to Kasma. He was scarcely prepared for the sight which lay beyond the door he opened now: it was in violent contrast with the mystic atmosphere of the other rooms. Operator 5 led his men cautiously into a large room, brilliantly lighted, equipped with numerous electrical devices—a laboratory!

IN SURPRISE, he noted a large tank into which heavily insulated cables led. In it, a bluish liquid was lapping with slow waves, as though it had recently been disturbed. On benches around the walls were numerous instruments employing the use of radio vacuum-tubes. Passing them, Operator 5 noted several amplifiers of tremendous power. Profoundly interested, he examined another machine, recognized it as an inscriber, of latest design, for making phonograph records. He turned from it to rows of cabinets built in the far wall.

Opening the doors, he found row after row of narrow compartments. In some of these were stored the huge wax master-records made on the recorder; in others were plates used for stamping; in still others were the completed records made on some flexible composition. His nerves tingling with a feeling of discovery, Jimmy Christopher drew out several of these; but they were without label of any kind. He hesitated, replaced them; he was turning to another door when a sound chilled and stopped him.

It was the prolonged, resonant, lingering note of a brazen gong. Its vibrant tone mingled with the weird music, and as it died away, the uncanny melody reached a new frenzy of clashing discords, quickening with a hysterical fervor. Operator 5 very quietly opened the far door of the laboratory, and the note-less music became louder, carrying a spellbinding enchantment.

Quickly, the Hidden Hundred following, Jimmy Christopher took long strides along another corridor. He paused facing fluttering red draperies. Cautiously he peered through into another narrow space. Its one side was a black wall; it's other, a long scarlet curtain which was wafting as if in a wind stirred by the play of supernatural forces. Jimmy Christopher led the way along it, signaling his skull-headed men to follow. The strange, hypnotic music continued its mind-numbing screech.

At a spot where the scarlet drapes overlapped, Jimmy Christopher carefully opened a crack and peered through. The sight which lay beyond caused a strange fascination in him. He looked into the center of the Temple of Kasma.

Red-draped walls enclosed the space of mystic worship; a scarlet ceiling covered it. Inside this place of crimson there were many persons. Kneeling and sitting on black cushions, scores of men and women were facing a cleared space at the head of the temple. They were sitting absolutely still, their widened eyes shining with a fanatical light. Utterly motionless, spellbound by the discordant singing of the unworldly music, they were waiting....

Again amazement filled Operator 5 as he recognized faces of important men and women. Among these worshipers at the feet of Kasma he saw men whose political power reached from coast to coast. He saw United States Senators and Representatives whose names were household words. Two men in military uniform he recognized as members of the Joint Board of the Army and Navy. He glimpsed two gray-haired women known for their wealth and their social prestige. He saw the faces of a score of young women and men celebrated on the stage and in motion-pictures. Within these red-draped walls were scores whose influence was powerful, whose following was of national scope—kneeling in worship to Kasma!

Now, while Operator 5 watched, while the chanting music swelled to sharper heights that rocked the mind, the red drapes at the opposite side of the temple stirred. Two Yellowese in black robes parted them. Men in single file entered the temple, each wearing the black clothing and the white stock of churchmen.

Jimmy Christopher peered at their faces in cold shock as their names sprang into his mind.

AT HEADQUARTERS Z-7 had received the startling report of the kidnapping of seven religious leaders within the city of New York. Now these seven were being led docilely, faces blank, eyes vacant, before Kasma's altar!

The black-robed Orientals who escorted them gave no signal, spoke no word; but as one body, the seven turned to face the scarlet drapes at the head of the temple. They remained motionless as the two Yellowese withdrew to the sides of the crimson space. It was as though the strange power of Kasma had robbed them of all volition, had rendered them responsive to commands which need not even be spoken! Operator 5 stared while the members of the Hidden Hundred waited, stationed behind the temple wall.

Suddenly the brazen note of the gong shook the air again. The instant it struck, the unearthly music faded to a whisper. As the lingering tones faded away, a hush filled the temple. A tense expectancy gleamed in the eyes of those who had come to worship. Then, slowly, the blood-red drapes fronting the cleared space stirred. Two long-nailed, yellow hands appeared, parted them. The power of a commanding presence was felt.

The Son of Kasma appeared.

The hypnotic effect of the whispering music, the interplay of dim light across the scarlet draperies, made of the Son of Kasma a being, who was scarcely visible, an ethereal presence which tricked vision. The color of the curtains blended with the hue of his majestic robe and the tone of his turban, so that he appeared translucent. He glided forward, every fascinated eye riveted upon him, his yellow hands tucked now inside the loose sleeves of his cloak, his saffron face contrasting with the red of the curtains.

Behind the drapes which concealed him and his men from the unholy congregation, Operator 5 felt the strange fascination of this mystic presence. Numbness filled his mind; a strange lethargy pervaded his body. He glanced back, saw his men peering about strangely, knew that they too were feeling the uncanny spell in the air—feeling it even though they could not see the Son of Kasma beyond the drapes!

Again the note of the gong vibrated in the air; and as it faded, the Son of Kasma's voice sounded, blending with it, rising from it, as though it were born of the brassy tone of the gong....

"The Son of Kasma looks upon his children of the true faith. The power of Kasma spreads its beneficence upon his followers. We are the saved—gazing now upon the leaders of the unbelieving lost."

The gleaming black eyes of the Son of Kasma passed slowly, glittering contemptuously, from face to face of the seven men of God.

His guttural intonations came: "We gaze upon the blind fools of a lost creed. Here we look upon those whom Kasma destroys because they will not heed his voice. He speaks from the vastness of eternal space, from beyond the ages when time began. His is the power which alone is greater than all his universes."

The seven churchmen listened with hypnotic fascination to the words of the Son of Kasma.

With startling swiftness, the red draperies were covered with leaping flames!

"Fools! A thousand years before your faith was known, men worshiped a deity closer to Kasma than your God. Out of Persia came Zoroaster, who laughed when he was born; who lived in the wilderness to strengthen himself for the task of purifying all religions. 'The mountain was consumed by fire' but Zoroaster alone escaped and 'spoke unto the multitude' for he was nearer than any man then to knowledge of Kasma.

"Now Kasma himself speaks to the multitude and commands worship. Now Kasma has wearied of untrue doctrines and futile faiths. Now Kasma has brought the blind of the earth before Aka, the Court of Judgment!"

THE VOICE of the Son of Kasma rose and fell weirdly, like the note-less melody that had filled the scarlet temple before.

"Man is warmed by the sun, yet the sun is but a dim spark in a universe spun out of nothingness by the power of Kasma. Man peers into the zenith through lenses and sees other suns so distant that centuries must pass before even their light may reach our puny sphere. Yet this distance, Kasma created, and across it his power flashes faster than the feeble mind of man can think. Man has dwelled upon earth by the grace of Kasma, but now he tires of ingratitude. Believe or meet your destruction! This is the one commandment revealed to you by the Son of Kasma!

"The Son of Kasma speaks!" Now the slanted, black eyes of the red-robed figure gleamed with deep fury. "The Son of Kasma, who was begot of the sea and the rocks, who is nurtured by the air and the light. He bids you worship him whose everlasting power is the Universal Force—worship him or fall before his might! He grants everlasting life to those who follow! He brings doom to those who serve false gods. He speaks, and his word destroys!"

Again the sharp, glittering eyes of the Son of Kasma passed from face to face of the seven Christian churchmen. They were still standing motionless, eyes fixed on the figure in the blood-red robe. A tremor passed through their bodies as the strange voice of the Son of Kasma exerted its unearthly power upon them.

"Give your worship to Kasma, or meet your doom!"

Now, faintly, as if from all the surrounding space, the strange toneless music issued again. If a signal had been uttered, no ear had heard it; but the red drapes at the side of the temple parted, and a single figure appeared. A man stepped forward slowly, his gaze upon the Son of Kasma; and at sight of him, Operator 5 felt a shock of surprise.

He knew, at his first glance, that his second squad of the Hidden Hundred had failed in their attempt to enter the temple; that they had been overpowered and captured; that now the uncanny power of Kasma held them helpless; for the man who appeared now was the member of the Hidden Hundred whom Jimmy Christopher had ordered to head the second squad.

Devoid of mask and gloves, X-15 slowly approached the Son of Kasma, his gaze never wavering. His face was lax, his eyes vacant. He moved like an automation while Operator 5 watched with growing horror. Jimmy Christopher's impulse was to leap forward, to attempt to tear X-15 away from the spell of the Son of Kasma; but an uncanny lethargy made his body heavy and his mind almost sluggish. He strove to combat the evil force which pervaded the temple while he watched X-15 pause facing the lean figure in the scarlet robe.

The voice of the Son of Kasma mingled again with the unworldly music. "You look upon one who refuses to believe in the power of Kasma. You see a blind, unhealing fool whose unfaithlessness arouses the wrath of Kasma. His doom will be yours unless you worship Kasma!"

Slowly, one yellow hand was drawn from the loose sleeve which concealed it. The yellow forefinger straightened, its long nail glittering, as it rose. Even the uncanny music became hushed as the Son of Kasma pointed a finger at X-15. The thin body of the red-robed figure towered, the slanting black eyes sparkled with live flame. "Kasma strikes! *Die!*"

X-15 dropped....

BEHIND THE red drapes Operator 5 stood spellbound with horror, with numb wonder. The music had ceased abruptly at the very moment when X-15 had crumpled to the floor; now utter silence filled the red temple. There was no sound until guttural, rumbling laughter came out of nowhere—laughter that mocked, that rose in power until it rocked the brains of those who heard—gloating laughter that came out of empty space, and vanished...!

Again, as though commanded by an unspoken order, one of the ministers moved. He stepped forward and bent over X-15; one of his colleagues came to his side. A quiet moment passed before they rose. Then a whisper came from the first, a word that passed breathily through the stillness:

"Dead!"

Two black-clad Orientals approached. They seized X-15's arms and legs, lifted him. They carried him to the red-draped wall and through it. Every person in the room watched, hushed by terror. The unearthly music blended out of the silence again after the curtains covered X-15. Out of it came the weird tones of the Son of Kasma:

"To those who worship him, Kasma grants eternal life. To those who are blind to him, he metes out doom!"

Operator 5 forced himself, with a tremendous effort, to turn from the curtain. The spell which numbed his mind and body was like the effect of a heavy, narcotic drug. Chilled by the sight he had seen, realizing that his men were in danger of succumbing to the evil power, he signaled them around him. They came almost unwillingly. The rising tone of the uncanny music covered Operator 5's tense whisper:

"Fight it! Don't let it get you! It means a living death at best for every one of you who yields. Those people we saw in the cells—they're sacrifices to Kasma. You'll find yourselves among them if you don't fight the spell of this temple!"

The masked eyes of the members of the Hidden Hundred peered at Operator 5 strangely. He noted anxiously that the evil effects were working as strongly upon his father as upon the others. His voice grew sharper, but he kept it desperately controlled, blanketed by the hypnotic cadences of the music:

"Listen to me! That man—the Son of Kasma—has murdered X-15—killed one of your comrades! Do you understand that? We want him as our prisoner! We've got to make him pay for that! We've got to stop him from enslaving the millions in this country. Scatter along this passage! When you hear my signal, close in on the Son of Kasma and—"

Operator 5 broke off abruptly when the uncanny music

ceased on a high, piercing note. Into the hush that followed it the voice of the red-robed man spoke.

"You dare not doubt! Kasma knows no mercy for those who doubt! He gives the first breath to babes as they are born, he takes the last breath from the aged as they die! He heeds naught but the belief of the heart. Young and old alike must worship his power—or meet their doom!"

Drawn by an uncanny terror, Operator 5 turned back to the curtain. He peered again through the drapes, into the temple. He saw that the curtains were again parting, that another figure was appearing. He saw, stepping through the red folds opposite, facing the Son of Kasma with eyes hypnotically fixed, a boy in worn clothing whose face was white beneath its spattering of freckles.

"Tim!" came in soundless horror from the lips of Operator 5. "Tim!"

WITH COLD fascination he gazed at Tim Donovan. The boy was moving toward the Son of Kasma as if drawn by a force greater than his own will. His steps were slow; his lips were working futilely in an effort to overcome the superhuman power that gripped him. His face did not show the ghastly, imbecilic laxity that Operator 5 had already seen on those struck by Kasma's power; he seemed to be in full possession of his senses, except that he was helpless to resist the Son of Kasma's unspoken commands.

Operator 5's hand grew cold on his automatic when Tim Donovan halted, facing the red-robed man. He turned the gun toward the Son of Kasma, but it required straining effort. He willed his finger to tighten on the trigger, but the response was laborious and exhausting. He puckered his lips to whistle the signal that would urge his men forward from their stations along the passage, but the very drawing of the breath was almost more than he could manage. Horrified by his own paralysis, Jimmy Christopher stared at Tim Donovan.

Into the silence of the red temple the voice of the Son of Kasma came: "Kasma asks if you believe!"

Tim Donovan's face went white with the effort he needed to answer: "No!"

Now the long-nailed, yellow hand of the red-robed figure slid slowly from the enveloping sleeve again. Now it began to rise, while the forefinger straightened toward the boy. Operator 5 had seen that lean finger with its glittering nail point death at X-15. Growing horror filled him as the hand raised slowly, deliberately, until the finger of doom was pointing directly between the trembling boy's eyes.

"Kasma—!"

Jimmy Christopher's gun spat. He had summoned all his strength into the simple movement of turning the automatic upon the Son of Kasma. The report was muffled and far-away in his own ears as the slug ripped through the curtain and sped over the heads of those who had come to see the fearful power of Kasma claim its sacrifices. Into that red and evil temple the roar of the gun carried a startling defiance.

The numbing effect in the air lay so powerfully upon Operator 5 that he had neglected the signal whistle. His voice was scarcely more than a whisper, though he meant it to be a ringing shout: "Get that man! Get the Son of Kasma!" He thrust himself forward through the red curtains, gripped by that horrible, baffling slowness which preys on one in dreams.

The Son of Kasma whirled at the report of the gun. His black-robed Yellowese spun toward Operator 5. Tim Donovan stood helpless, merely staring, unable even to speak the name of his friend. Again Operator 5 attempted to shout: "Get that man!" as he strode toward the Son of Kasma, each step an effort, each move exhausting him. Vaguely, he saw the skull-masked members of the Hidden Hundred breaking through the curtain, moving with the same terrifying lethargy.

From the lips of the Son of Kasma came a high-pitched screech.

"Aka!"

A muffled roar instantly followed. The low, ominous rolling sound came from all quarters at once. The scarlet drapes billowed out with a blasting of air that shocked through the entire temple. As the curtains wafted, red tongues of fire appeared near the floor and rapidly traveled upward. With startling swiftness the red of the draperies was blotted over by the brighter crimson of leaping flame!

OPERATOR 5 flung himself toward the Son of Kasma as the fire sheeted up to wall the room. Instantly the temple became a blazing hell. Walls and ceiling alike flowed with the blinding flames that radiated from every point. In the glare, the unholy congregation began to scatter wildly. The shouted command of the Son of Kasma had brought a burst of guttural voices from recesses beyond the curtains, and suddenly a horde of black-cloaked Yellowese appeared.

The skull-masked Hidden Hundred fought their way through the mobbing worshipers, struggled against the binding spell of the flaming temple, while Jimmy Christopher propelled himself slowly through hot air that seemed to have the thickness of oil. In the frantic confusion, his first thought was for Tim Donovan. He saw the boy striving to tear away, forcing himself into a run toward the front of the temple. Two black-gowned Yellowese leaped after him and Operator 5 shifted desperately to follow.

"Get that man!" he attempted to shout again to his men. "Get him!"

But the horrifying, nightmarish hindrances of Kasma's power became even still more overpowering as Jimmy Christopher tried to follow Tim Donovan. The boy flung himself into the flames near the wall and plunged through a door. The moves of the two Yellowese who sprang after him were amazingly swift. Operator 5 glanced back to see his men striving to reach the Son of Kasma in the turmoil. He pushed himself on with all his strength toward the door that Tim Donovan had entered.

The Temple of Kasma was already a flaming furnace filled with terrified worshipers struggling against their lethargy to reach the hidden exits. The roaring of the fire was a constant deafening thunder; the heat was suffocating, the glare blinding. Operator 5 thrust himself with all his leaden strength through a flaring sheet of fire, into the room which Tim Donovan had entered.

Once he was past the doorway, some of the stupefying effect

in the air left him, but his movements were still slow, his mind still numb. He glimpsed Tim Donovan crouched against one wall, struggling breathlessly with something which Operator 5 could not see. The two Yellowese were advancing on the boy, each gripping a huge automatic. Operator 5 dragged his own gun level. Desperately, terrorized by the hypnotic weakness which filled him, he pulled the trigger.

The blast of the gun was almost lost in the thunderous roaring of flames in the temple. The bullet wrung a scream from one of the slant-eyed men, sprawled him back with gun-arm broken. The other whirled and the muzzle of his gun became a black mouth yawning into Operator 5's eyes. Jimmy Christopher fired again as the other weapon spat. A sharp, stinging pain shot along his right arm, flashing from the torn flesh where the bullet had struck, and his paralyzed fingers dropped his automatic.

Suddenly Operator 5 heard a glad cry from Tim Donovan; suddenly he felt the paralyzing force vanish. In a second, Jimmy Christopher came capable of swift action, clear thought. He sensed that Tim Donovan had done something to rescue him from the deadly effects, even as he reached for his fallen automatic with his left hand. A savage thrust sprawled him away from it. He sprang up to see the wounded Yellowese gliding toward him, automatic leveled in his other hand for a final shot—saffron finger tightening for a pull of the trigger which would send a bullet drilling through his heart.

Operator 5's left hand flashed to the buckle of his belt. As he leaped aside, the gun blasted, and a slug ripped through his coat, under the arm and beside the heart. His left hand swung out;

his belt flicked from its loops and flew through the air. Jimmy Christopher's rapier of Toledo steel appeared glittering in the light. The weapon, which he always wore in its flexible scabbard circled around his waist, twinkled a deadly defiance in the flickering of spreading flames as he lunged at the Yellowese.

SPARKLING STEEL played upon the gun in the hand of the black-cloaked man. Magical power snatched the weapon from the long-nailed fingers. The Oriental sprang forward with a cry of rage, fingers spread to grip Jimmy Christopher's throat in a deadly clutch. That move was his doom. A brief tremor passed along the steel of Jimmy Christopher's épée as it plunged through the body of the Yellowese. He drew back, and the steel glittered red. The disciple of Kasma slid to the floor and lay against the door-sill over which voracious flame-tongues were licking.

"Jimmy!"

Tim Donovan sprang toward Operator 5. Jimmy Christopher cautioned, "Steady, old timer!" For the first time, he had an opportunity to make a swift examination of the room. He noted that one wall was a switchboard on which huge copper blades were shining. On stout shelves which occupied half the room were score upon score of storage batteries connected in series. From them, heavy cables led toward the giant knife-switches on the panel. Again, they snake through insulators in the wall.

"Tim—are you all right?"

"Okay, Jimmy!"

"After me, Tim!"

Operator 5 peered out the door and saw that the Temple of

Kasma was a place of roaring flames. He could not doubt that the fire had been started at the Son of Kasma's shouted signal. A touch of a switch, carrying electrical impulses along concealed wiring to fuses attached to stores of combustibles in the walls, had set the great room ablaze in a second. Now he saw that it was a veritable furnace through which escape was impossible.

"This way, Jimmy!" Tim Donovan had sprung to a door at the side of the room. Operator 5 thrust through after him. Startled, he saw that this room was equipped as a sending and receiving wireless station. It was from here, then, that Tim Donovan managed to send the message which had first urged Operator 5 to plan the attack on the Temple of Kasma. As he passed the installation, Jimmy Christopher noted that its switches were all on; he sensed that a message had flashed out over a hidden antenna only a few seconds previous.

"On the roof!" The husky shout carried to Operator 5 through the roaring of the flames. "They went up to the roof!"

A man in skull mask cried the information through a door that was a square of billowing flame. Operator 5 signaled Tim Donovan to his side, retreated for a run that would carry him past the blistering barrier. A glance out the window filled him with amazement.

A short time ago, when he had made the first move to enter this secret citadel of evil worship, the sun had been shining brightly. Now a veritable torrent of rain was pouring down the panes. Water was lashing savagely over the glass in a solid deluge, he could not see through.

"With me, Tim!" Operator 5 commanded.

Side by side they rushed through the flaming doorway. They sprinted along a corridor, led by the man in the skull mask who had shouted the warning. Another door gave onto a flight of steps which angled upward. Down them, water was streaming. Jimmy Christopher urged Tim Donovan ahead as they hurried up. They stepped out of a superstructure on the roof—into the blinding fury of the rain.

WATER WAS pouring out of the sky, and as it fell, it sparkled with the light of the sun shining into it from above! The deluge was so thick that the edges of the roof could not be seen. It was blinding and suffocating—an onslaught of water roaring like a Niagara. Below the roof, flames were sheeting up; from above it the flood was descending; and at that moment Operator 5 felt more than ever before that he was in the grip of a supernatural power.

Dim figures were struggling through the sluicing wash of water. Out of the roar of the rain a voice carried to Jimmy Christopher. "They're gone! They rushed up here, and now they're gone! They couldn't have got down—they couldn't have gotten away—but there's no sign of them!"

Operator 5 recognized the strained voice of John Christopher. "Make sure of that! If you're certain they've escaped, order all men down the fire-escape!"

He fought his way through the staggering downpour to the cornice, searching for the means of leaving the roof. Ex-Operator Q-6 gripped his arm. "We've already made sure! Not one of them is up here! We saw them come up—they locked the door on us, but we broke it down—but by the time we got into the roof, the rain was blinding! I tell you—"

"Order all men down!"

Through the rumble of the rain and the growling of the fire, the shrill shrieking of fire-sirens was drilling. Operator 5 realized that the alarm would soon surround the building with firemen and police. It meant capture to the Hidden Hundred, death for all members of the outlaw organization who might be arrested. Again he ordered sharply:

"All men down!"

Tim Donovan clung to the cornice, choking in the downpour, and caught only a glimpse of Operator 5 turning away. Through the blinding rain the members of the Hidden Hundred struggled. They legged over the cornice, onto the top platform of the fire-escape, uncertain of their own movements in the pelting flood. John Christopher's shouts brought all the men to the platform. He followed Tim Donovan and was the last to go over. As the boy seized the railing and peered through the sheeting water he called frantically:

"Dad! Jimmy hasn't come back! He hasn't come back!"

"I know, Tim!" John Christopher choked out. "He went down into the building!"

The boy screeched through the shrilling of the fire-sirens. "I'm going to find him! I won't go without—"

"It's hopeless, Tim! Jimmy will get out alone all right! Go down, boy! This roof is going to drop in a minute—"

"I'm going back—!"

Tim attempted to fight his way past John Christopher. His

hard hands clamped to the rungs; he would not let go when Operator 5's father attempted to pull him free. Desperately and deliberately, John Christopher struck a powerful, slapping blow across the boy's face. The stinging power of it sagged Tim against the ladder. Ex-Operator Q-6 seized him, dragged him off. Holding the boy close, he began descending the ladders while the rain beat viciously upon him, while his heart pounded heavily with dread for his son, Operator 5.

TIM DONOVAN struggled to free himself; he sobbed frantically in wild protest; but John Christopher held him securely until they left the last ladder. They went across ground that was flowing like a river. In the deluge, sirens were still shrieking; fire-engines were clattering down the flooded streets toward the building. While the torrent beat upon it, flame continued to roar from the top windows. And under the gray cascade of water, the members of the Hidden Hundred were scattering.

Close by the bank of the East River, Tim Donovan and John Christopher paused, whipped by the rain, peering back at the glare of the flame. They could see nothing except the falling gray sheets of water all around them; yet above, dimly, a glow told them that the sun was shining. The Niagara seemed to increase in ferocity; and then, abruptly, the downpour diminished in intensity!

In a few moments the last drop fell; the sun beamed upon a flowing earth; gutters ran deep with water while flames blazed far above the streets and mystified fire crews went into action.

"Jimmy!"

Tim Donovan broke into a run toward the drenched figure

that was hurrying along the bank. Operator 5's clothing trailed water as he came to a breathless stop. He had removed his mask; his hair and eyebrows were singed; his clothing was reddened by the blood flowing from his wounds. He stumbled to a stop, choked with the sting of the fumes in his lungs.

"I'm—okay—old-timer!"

Operator 5 gasped the words, even as he peered around. "Thank God our men have scattered, Dad! The Son of Kasma slipped us—but that temple of evil is doomed!"

"How they were able to vanish off that roof is beyond me! That devil *must* have some supernatural power!"

"Jimmy!" Tim exclaimed in amazement. "What've you got there?"

"I went back for these, Tim," Operator 5 answered in an exhausted whisper.

Under one arm he was carrying a number of large red discs of red composition, each the thickness of cardboard. He had dared return to the laboratory of the temple in order to seize these huge and unlabeled phonograph records. He held them tightly as he supported himself and peered up at the building which was flaming like a huge torch.

"They may mean nothing, but—"

A terrific, roaring burst of sound blanketed his words. It thundered out of the blue sky—that same uncanny burst that Operator 5 had already twice heard. It rolled from empty space, split into countless echoes, and vanished in the roaring of the flames that were consuming an unholy temple.

It was the mocking laughter of Kasma…!

CHAPTER 6
FATHOMLESS SILENCE

OPERATOR 5 stood before the electric phonograph and carefully placed the red, fifteen-inch record on the turntable. It was one of the dozen he had seized from the laboratory in the hidden temple of Kasma. He inserted a new needle in the pick-up and poised it carefully over the first groove. He did not know what strange sounds he might find recorded on these mysterious records; yet he was not prepared for the result of this test.

No sound whatever issued from the instrument!

Curiously Jimmy Christopher checked all adjustments. He turned the volume control to its highest point. He made sure that the phonograph was in normal operating order, and started the red record again. But again, as the needle traced the grooves, Operator 5 heard absolutely no sound issue from the reproducer.

"Gee, Jimmy!" Tim Donovan exclaimed. "That's funny! They wouldn't make a record without any sound, on it at all, would they?"

"These are important, Tim—I'm certain of that," Operator 5 answered slowly. "I think that if we solve the mystery of these records, we'll be close to knowing the secret of the power of Kasma, but—"

His voice faded as he exchanged the first disc for another. Again the needle traced the grooves without result. One after another, Operator 5 tried the records, until he had tested every one he had brought from the hidden temple; but he heard nothing from the amplifying horn. Not content, he started the last again, and allowed it to continue its soundless revolutions while he stood in thought.

He had hurried from the scene of the fire directly to Headquarters HN. There the Intelligence surgeon had treated his wounds. He had made a quick report to Z-7, who had listened gravely and with scarcely a comment. Immediately, he had come to this brownstone house in the East Forties. It was the house of John Christopher and Tim Donovan; in the lexicon of the Intelligence it was designated Address Y. Here Operator 5 had quickly changed to dry clothing, eager to hear what the huge records might reveal of the secret of Kasma.

Yet now, as Operator 5 stood listening, he heard not the slightest whisper of sound from the electric phonograph, though the volume control was full on and the device was in perfect working order.

Tim Donovan exclaimed: "What does it all mean?"

John Christopher asked quickly: "Is it possible that after all the man who calls himself the Son of Kasma does possess some strange supernatural power?"

"No, Dad," Operator 5 answered briskly. "There's a logical, scientific explanation for everything that's happened—we simply haven't found the secret yet. We've got to find it! We've got to learn the nature of this devilish force of Kasma—or it will doom the United States!"

A girl was standing beside Operator 5, her clear blue eyes searching his. She was his age, and strikingly pretty. Forthright, courageous, self-reliant, Diane Elliot had earned herself an enviable reputation as a special reporter for the far-flung Amalgamated Press Service. They had faced the dangers of many cases together. Operator 5 had repeatedly called upon Diane and Tim for extraordinary services which could not be detailed to known members of the Intelligence, and no danger had made them hesitate. He knew he could rely upon both of them to the limit.

The girl asked Jimmy Christopher anxiously: "Are you sure of that, Jimmy? The cult of Kasma has grown to such a dangerous scope?"

OPERATOR 5 drew folded flimsies from his pocket—communications he had brought with him from Headquarters HN—and passed them to the girl.

"Read them, Di," he said quietly. "They will answer your question. The power of Kasma has been operating secretly for months, and now it has launched into a destructive campaign on a gigantic scale. If it succeeds, it will become a power controlling the whole nation—the government, with all its wealth—and it will enslave all the people."

Diane rapidly read the first, brief reports. They were instances of the disappearance of Intelligence men, of the strange deaths of undercover operators and Christian ministers; they cited cases of strange amnesia from coast to coast, of scores of prominent men and women, in the church and the Intelligence service, suddenly becoming maniacs. It was a longer report that brought a sharper chill to her heart:

... HN-NY... SPECIAL REPORT CONDITIONS
MIDWEST FOLLOWING INSTRUCTIONS... MYSTIC

CULT SPREADING OVER ENTIRE DROUGHT SECTION... THOUSANDS SWARMING TO KASMA... FAMILIES PENNILESS FROM DONATIONS TO MYSTIC LEADERS... HUGE SECTION UNDER MYSTIC'S CONTROL... ALL ROADS GUARDED... IMPOSSIBLE TO PENETRATE INTO THIS SECRET STRONGHOLD OF KASMA... TEMPLE ERECTED IN DESERT FROM WHICH LEADERS OPERATE... DOING OUR UTMOST TO GATHER INFORMA-TION BUT PROGRESS IS HOPELESS... MYSTERI-OUS DEATHS, AMNESIA AND MADNESS REDUCE AGENTS IN MIDWEST HEADQUARTERS TO HAND-FUL... FOR GOD'S SAKE SEND MEN... TK....

Operator 5 had been watching the red record revolve under the needle of the electric phonograph. Now, as it reached the last groove, having placed to the end without a sound he turned the power off. To Diane he passed another flimsy with the cryptic remark:

"This may also have a connection."

The designation at the end of the message declared it to have been sent from the seat of government of the great Yellow Empire:

... HN-NY THRU WDC-13... STRANGE AGITA-TION DISTURBING ROYAL HOUSE OF YELLOW EMPIRE... REIGNING FAMILY IN SECLUSION ALL PUBLIC APPEARANCES CANCELLED... LEADING STATESMEN FRANTIC... UNKNOWN

CRISIS OF VITAL IMPORTANCE TO EMPIRE HAS OCCURRED... DESPERATE EFFORTS BEING MADE TO KEEP IT SECRET... INVESTIGATION PROMISES NO RESULTS... TYE....

Operator 5, gazing at Tim Donovan, asked the boy quietly: "Will you tell me again, Tim, exactly what happened when you followed the car of the Son of Kasma to the hidden temple?"

"Sure, Jimmy!" the boy assented; and his eyes widened as he recalled the amazing episode. "I can't explain all of it—I only know that nothing like it ever happened to me before."

The boy rapidly repeated his account. When Operator 5's car had crashed on the Drive, following the destruction of the great church, Tim Donovan had been thrown out almost unhurt. Though dazed, he had thought only of continuing the chase of the Son of Kasma. A taxi had carried him swiftly after the fleeing car to the apartment building which stood at the river's edge on the East Side.

HE HAD dared enter the building, and once he stepped into an elevator, he had sensed that he was trapped. He had been seized by two Yellowese and taken into a room high in the building. There he had been held prisoner, alone. After a while, he had been taken out and, to his dismay, placed in a huge cage like a wild animal. Held there in a draped room, he had experienced the first strange effects of the power of Kasma.

The Son of Kasma had appeared and merely looked at him. A paralytic numbness had overcome the boy. He had struggled against it with all his will. Playing a desperate gamble, he had pretended that the weird effects were much stronger than they really were. Simulating a hypnotic stupor, he had been taken from the cage. The Son of Kasma had commanded him to wait, and had withdrawn.

"He left me because a message was brought to him. It was about the seven ministers who had been kidnapped and taken to the temple. They thought my memory was gone, and I wouldn't remember what was said, but I was doing my best to fight that power. I—I'm sure of this, Jimmy, and yet it seems like a dream—something that didn't really happen."

The boy's voice sounded far-away when he continued, as though he were laboriously drawing details from dim recesses of his mind. He explained that immediately he was left alone, he had stolen from the room into the adjoining chambers. He had seen enough to be convinced that the huge bank of storage batteries and the great switchboard had something to do with the power of Kasma. Then, finding the wireless installation, he had attempted to send a message in the special code.

His absence was discovered; he was seized, dragged away before he could complete the message. The Son of Kasma had issued angry commands in Yellowese and again Tim had been thrown into the cage. This time, all his efforts to combat the weird power were fruitless. It had thrown him into a strange passive state, so that he could not think, could only respond unquestioningly to commands.

"But they didn't speak the commands, Jimmy!" the boy exclaimed. "The Son of Kasma just looked at me, and I knew what he was thinking. I understood perfectly what he wanted me to do, and I had to obey—but he didn't utter a word!"

Operator 5 observed quietly: "Thought transference—not an unusual phenomenon of hypnosis. But the spell of Kasma is not hypnotism—I am positive of that."

Diane Elliot asked anxiously: "Why are you sure, Jimmy?"

"Hypnotism is not the uncanny power it is thought to be, Di," he explained. "People in general believe a great deal of nonsense about it. It is merely a condition of extreme susceptibility to suggestion brought about by concentration. No person can be hypnotized against his will. Tim could easily have resisted any attempt to hypnotize him—but he could not resist the spell of Kasma."

"Then what is that spell, Jimmy?" John Christopher asked with deep concern.

OPERATOR 5 gestured hopelessly. "Electricity has something to do with it—but it is not electrical in character, for my tests at the Church of the Divine proved that. It is not an electrical phenomenon, yet that power ceased immediately, Tim got to the panel and threw off the great master-switch. Perhaps the switch controlled a ventilating system that was circulating a stupefying gas throughout the temple, but that's only a guess and it might be wrong. I intend to make further tests—"

Jimmy Christopher's voice faded as he stood in thought; and when he resumed, his words were brisk and clear.

"There are other strange things about the use of the power of Kasma. Why wasn't it turned upon me and my men to destroy us? Why did the Yellowese use automatics to fight me, instead of that mystic power? Why was not the power used to destroy the temple instead of fire? The answers to those questions are important."

"Perhaps that last," Jimmy," Diane spoke up, "it was because Kasma would not destroy his own temple when his power is used only to destroy those who refuse to believe in him."

"Yes," Operator 5 agreed. "But the others—"

The ring of the telephone turned Operator 5 away. Over the line came a quiet "HN calling." The voice of Z-7 followed, throaty and low:

"Operator 5, I have been checking your report on the hidden Temple of Kasma. The fire has been put out and an investigation is being made. There are many dead in the ruins, and some of the charred bodies have been found in cells. You spoke of seeing the seven kidnapped ministers there. They have not returned to their homes; it's certain that they are among the dead."

Operator 5 listened gravely.

"As for the congregation, most of them escaped apparently under the cover of the rain. That damnable downpour has thrown the Bureau of Meteorology into confusion. They can't account for it. Torrents fell over an area of the East Side and in Brooklyn, but the rest of the city was not touched. I'm being forced to the conclusion that whatever this damnable power is we're fighting, it's a hopeless task."

"I'm far from giving up, Chief," Jimmy Christopher answered tartly. "I still believe that the secret can be learned and the power of Kasma destroyed."

"There is no way of fighting it except through the Intelligence, and our force is seriously crippled. What few men we have are still kept out of action by orders of the Secretary. I tell you, the situation is absolutely hopeless!"

"Chief," Jimmy Christopher answered, "I can't concede that. I'm sure that the power of Kasma will strike again—and each time it strikes, we can, if we try, get closer to the secret. It means horrible destructions and suffering, but there is no other way. When another report reaches you, Chief, please let me know at once, here at Address Y."

"I will, my boy. I have informed the Secretary of your move, because my duty compels it. He has the report under consideration now. I am afraid he'll take drastic action against you for daring to disobey his orders."

"I am ready to take the consequences, chief," Jimmy Christopher declared, grimly.

HE TURNED from the instrument, his eyes gravely dark. Unconsciously his hand strayed to the little golden ornament on his watch-chain—a skull cunningly fashioned of gold, its eyes glittering red gems. His shoulders sagged with despair as he gazed at the mysterious records and he spoke quietly.

"There is a diabolical purpose behind this spread of the cult of Kasma. Religion strikes deep into the human heart, and Kasma embraces all creeds. It is a worship of cosmic forces—forces that play through all the space of the universe, creating as well as destroying—forces which are timeless and merciless. The belief that only faith in Kasma can save the world from annihilation will bring the whole nation, the whole earth, to bow before Kasma—and the Son of Kasma will rule supreme."

John Christopher declared in bewilderment: "I cannot see

how any natural power can achieve all these results, Jimmy—how any one thing can crash great buildings to the ground, cause torrents of rain to pour from the sky, kill men instantly, make them mad, render them helpless, destroy their minds. It must be a greater power than any man ever controlled before—it *must* be a true cosmic force which *will* destroy the world at the command of the Son of Kasma unless we—"

Operator 5's voice crackled as he interrupted. "You must not believe that, Dad! You must not let yourself think it for one moment! That very attitude is enslaving hundreds of thousands of people today. It will enslave the whole country if it isn't stopped in time! There is no strange cosmic power involved.

"The cult of Kasma is, instead, the gigantic conspiracy of a group of mystics to seize upon the great wealth of the United States, to conquer this nation and make it their own through the power of deep-rooted terror!"

A tense moment followed Operator 5's outburst. It was Tim Donovan who spoke first, quietly: "Jimmy, I've been with you in this from the beginning, and I know you're right. If it was some super natural power, it wouldn't stop at the throw of a switch. But Jimmy, you can't let it get you, either. It's preying on your mind—you've got to stop thinking about it…."

Operator 5 smiled. "You're right, Tim. It's hit me harder than anything else ever has, because it's so baffling—and yet I know there's a simple explanation for it. All right, old-timer. We'll take our minds off it with a few feats of magic. What do you say?"

Tim exclaimed: "It's been a long time since you showed me a new trick. The ones you do look like the workings of a supernatural power, too, but they've all got a very simple explanation—just as the power of Kasma must have."

"Exactly!" Jimmy Christopher exclaimed with a smile.

HE TURNED on the radio, adjusted it to a musical program, then took a pack of cards from the desk. While Tim and Diane and John Christopher watched with deep interest, he selected the four queens and the four kings and discarded the rest. He displayed them, fanned in one hand, and was about to speak when the music of the radio ceased and an announcer's voice sounded:

"At the conclusion of the present program, ladies and gentlemen, the Reverend Hugh Dodson will address you over a coast-to-coast hook-up on a subject vital to the nation. His speech will be a plea to the people to turn from the mystic faith which is now sweeping the country. As spokesman for every church and every religious leader of the United States the Reverend Dodson deserves your uninterrupted attention. Please stand by for this historic address, which will originate in the International Broadcasting Studios in New York and be heard by all the world."

Operator 5's eyes narrowed in thought. But Tim Donovan urged him to continue with the feat of magic. Again displaying the four kings and the four queens, he gathered them in a packet and placed them on the table. "Now, Tim," he directed, "cut them as many times as you wish."

The eager boy complied, cutting the packet repeatedly, until he was certain that the eight cards were thoroughly mixed. Operator 5 then took them, placed them behind his back. Talking quietly, explaining that the kings and queens were magic cards which somehow could never be successfully separated, he brought two of the cards forward from behind his back, holding them in one hand.

They were the king and queen of spades.

Again, while Tim wondered, Operator 5 brought a pair of the cards forward, and this time they were the king and queen of diamonds. Next he produced the pair of hearts together, lastly the pair of clubs. "You see," he said with a smile, "they stick together through thick and thin."

"I don't see how you did that, Jimmy!" the boy exclaimed.

"And there's more," Operator 5 chuckled as he continued with the trick. He gathered the cards into a packet, and again Tim Donovan cut it. Operator 5 placed them behind his back again. This time he brought both hands forward at the same time, holding four cards in each. The amazed Tim saw that in one hand Operator 5 held all the kings, and in the other all the queens!

"I'm stumped!" the boy blurted. "Unless you've got some way of knowing which is which by the sense of feel, Jimmy!"

Operator 5 allowed Tim to examine the cards thoroughly, but the boy found absolutely nothing suspicious about them. He gave up, completely baffled, and Jimmy Christopher smilingly said:

"Before I tell you how to do that one, Tim, let me show you another. It's a variation of the old choose-a-card routine, but an especially good one." He shuffled the kings and queens back into the deck as he spoke. "These, you see, are thoroughly mixed. Now I give them to you."

Operator 5 directed Tim to cut the deck and lift a small number from the top of lower half, not more than a dozen cards. This done, Tim counted the number he had taken and noted the bottom card of the group. He placed his packet on top of the deck.

Operator 5 took the pack. He dealt a number of cards on the table-top in a spiral. Tim counted twenty of them. Jimmy Christopher's hands hovered over them, then he lifted one of the cards. It was an eight.

"That," he said quietly, "is the number of cards you selected."

"Right!" Tim exclaimed as Operator 5 scattered the cards about on the table.

They were moved in a thoroughly confusing fashion, all face down. At last Jimmy Christopher picked one up. "What was the card you had on the bottom of the bunch you took, Tim?" he asked, and the boy answered, "The ten of spades." Operator 5 promptly displayed the card he had already selected—and it was the ten of spades!

"Gee, you've fooled me completely!" the boy exclaimed. "I can't guess how you did either of them. What's the secret? You'll tell me, won't you?"

"Certainly, Tim," Operator 5 agreed.

"They're both very simple. The first—"

HE BROKE off as another announcement came from the radio, and listened. "We bring you now, ladies and gentlemen of the radio audience, the Reverend Hugh Dodson, who will speak to you on behalf of the federated churches of the United States. Over this nation-wide hook-up, the Reverend Dodson will address his plea for the salvation of Christianity in the United States. He comes now to the microphone to warn the nation against the danger of the mysticism which is sweeping the country. The Reverend Dodson—"

The ring of the telephone bell brought a sharp pang of disappointment to Tim Donovan, for to him it meant a delay in the explanation of the two card tricks. Operator 5, lifting the receiver, heard a grave voice say "The Department of State, calling from Washington." The tones that followed were heavy, ominous.

"The Secretary speaking, Operator 5. I have just been informed by Z-7 of your insubordination. I intend to deal with it drastically. I order you to report to me in Washington at the soonest possible moment."

Coldly Operator 5 answered, "Yes, sir!"

"That's all."

The terse message filled Jimmy Christopher with dread. He turned gravely from the telephone; and a sudden crackling sound from the radio startled him.

The smooth, pleading tones of the Reverend Dodson, one of the greatest religious leaders in the nation, were drowned out by the roar. When it passed, the voice was a jarring, strident discord; the words were almost unintelligible. Suddenly, in the midst of a sentence, the minister's voice vanished and another rang out of the radio—high-pitched, frantic.

"Ladies and gentlemen! We are obliged to terminate this broadcast because of conditions beyond our control. We hope to resume—"

Operator 5 scarcely heard the repeated ringing of the telephone in the deafening clatter that filled the room. Then, suddenly, even that din vanished.

Only the faint hum of the carrier-wave issued from the loudspeaker as Jimmy Christopher lifted the receiver. The voice on the line was Z-7's—strained, rasping, expressing utter consternation and desperation.

"Operator 5! That damnable power is striking again! It is hitting the tower of the International Broadcasting Building! The report has just come in that the skyscraper is going to pieces right now!"

"Chief!" Operator 5's voice snapped. "Order all our men to that spot! You've got to disregard the Secretary's orders now! Send them into the streets around that building with bottles—as many of any kind they can find—empty and corked. They've got to take samples of the air in that region. It's an important chance, Chief!"

Operator 5 whirled from the telephone, snatched up his hat. Tim Donovan bounded to the door with him; Diane Elliot and John Christopher sprang up to follow. As they raced down the stairs to the street entrance, booming tones suddenly issued from the radio in the living-room. The commanding voice brought them all to a sharp stop, and they listened in amazement.

"The Son of Kasma speaks!"

Operator 5 waited to hear no more. He sped from the door, with Tim and the girl and his father, toward the powerful Diesel-engined roadster which was waiting at the curb....

"Karma strikes!" Destruction cleaved the sheer, high walls!

CHAPTER 7
BRINGER OF TERROR

A SCENE stranger than any living person had ever witnessed before was occurring in the streets surrounding the rearing tower of the International Broadcasting Corporation.

In the streets flanking the majestic structure, thousands of people were strolling; walking to and from nearby Broadway, in and out of scores of restaurants and stores in the district. While the sun set in glowing, red flame—as the moment approached when the Reverend Dodson's broadcast was to begin—they felt a strange sensation creep over them; they saw a strange procession passing slowly along Fifth Avenue.

The effects of that weird lethargy were felt the length of the broad thoroughfare and in the cross-streets branching from it. Men and women paused in wonderment as a heaviness of mind and body settled over them. They peered around blankly as if reality had ceased to exist, as if the buildings and the beings around them were parts of a dream which all of them shared. A hush settled; within it, thousands stood, held motionless with a strange hypnotic stupor. They gazed dully at the numerous cars which crawled to a standstill....

In all the length of the avenue, only three automobiles moved now. Thousands of eyes followed as they slowed in a cleared intersection. The traffic officer stationed there stood transfixed; he made no move—his eyes did not even express mild wonder—as a strange figure stepped from the second of the sedans.

A lean man, clad in scarlet robe, wearing a scarlet turban, took gliding steps along the street. His black, slanted eyes gleamed in his yellow face and reflected the crimson glare of the sunset. His long-nailed hands were curled within the loose sleeves of his robe as he turned to face the rearing, white-stone spire. Then slowly, he withdrew one hand, raised it, pointing his finger.

Toward the towering spire he pointed the slim finger of doom!

"Kasma strikes!"

The hush grew deeper. It was a silence that seemed to quiet even the normal hum of the city around the great building. Then, almost inaudibly at first, a tremor began shaking the air. The ground beneath the feet of the awed spectators began to tremble. The quaking of the giant edifice was a motion which was at first invisible. The destructive power of Kasma showed itself suddenly when a mass of stonework tore from the topmost point of the skyscraper and hurtled into the street.

NOW THE great building was visibly trembling on its foundations. It had become a quivering shell endangering thousands of terrorized men and women inside. They mobbed out of studios, ran screaming along corridors which were shaking all around them. Plaster was falling; ceilings were tumbling down; elevators were jammed in twisting shafts, and stairways were clotted with those frantically stampeding from the doomed structure. On many floors of the great building, men and women went mad with fear as the power of Kasma seized upon them.

Destruction cleaved at the sheer, high walls. Tremendous blocks of stone broke away and hurtled into streets already strewn with debris. Great steel girders knifed through the crumbling walls; the whole framework was shaking more violently with every new moment. The downpour of falling stone from the buckling walls became a deadly avalanche raining into the streets. The crushed fragments of a great building piled high.

The turmoil which filled the skyscraper had disrupted the operation of the coast-to-coast network completely. Technicians fled their posts as rooms collapsed around them. Thousands of miles of wires went silent, even though the connections were not broken. Huge conduits writhed in the quaking walls though they remained intact. The network remained, but the human element which controlled it was swept away by strangling terror. Only silent carrier waves radiated from more than a hundred antennae, scattered over the country—until, suddenly, the haunting, hollow tones of the mystic sounded:

"The Son of Kasma speaks!"

Millions of times the words were reproduced, by millions of radios throughout the nation. The multitude had gathered to hear the plea of a great religious leader; now they listened with awe to the baleful tones of the Son of Kasma. They listened as though these were words springing disembodied out of cosmic space!

"The Son of Kasma speaks! Kasma ordains the destruction of all who blind themselves to his power! Kasma commands the worship of his goodness while he destroys the evil of faithlessness and corruption!"

Even while the mysterious words flashed across the nation,

the gigantic structure in New York City was crashing to the street!

"The Son of Kasma, born of the sea and the rocks, nurtured by the air and the light, is the voice of the everlasting power which demands the trial of the world before Aka, the Court of Judgment! No force can equal the strength of Kasma! It turns upon the earth with wrath and fury for the corrupt and faithless, with life and bliss for the faithful. The Day of Doom is at hand!

"Raise your eyes into the space of the sky, where Kasma dwells. Harken to the voice of his son! Lost are the evil! The sinful will be swept away. Selfish government will be destroyed. Blind leaders will meet eternal doom before Aka. The end of the world is here for all who turn their eyes from Kasma!"

THE DEATH groans of a great building sounded over Manhattan while the awesome words reached the entire nation. The denuded steel skeleton of the skyscraper warped and swayed. Like a great thing wracked by the agonies of death, it tottered on its base. Second by second brought complete dissolution nearer—while the voice of Kasma's Son was multiplied millions of times in the fear-stricken homes of America.

"These benefactions Kasma promises those who live in his worship: Freedom from all the evil practices of a depraved mankind; annihilation of greedy political leaders; the inexorable sentence of Aka upon corrupt government. All are doomed—all save the worshipers of Kasma!"

A terrific roar rumbled over New York City as the last, awful concussion ripped through the skyscraper. Its steel framework burst asunder. Jagged fragments of girders flew through the sky, hurled mightily by an invisible power. The rooted foundations of the great building tore from solid stone and bounded in the air— to crush the smaller surrounding buildings. For many blocks around, awesome destruction spread, as the majestic tower of stone and steel became a wretched mass of chaotic wreckage.

Now the stupefying spell which had held the thousands motionless in the street suddenly broke. The dreamy stupor lifted from their eyes. Realization exploded in them.

Women screamed; men shouted hoarsely as they mobbed away from the ghastly scene. Cars spurted now along the streets like frightened rabbits. A wild mob fled, frantically seeking escape from the power that had struck—that might strike again at any instant! Through it, horns blaring, a fleet of powerful cars came from the opposite direction, massing toward the spot where chaotic horror littered the pavements.

The men who leaped out were Intelligence operators acting under Jimmy Christopher's orders as relayed by Z-7. Their actions might have seemed mad, to those who could not understand, but they went about their task with grim gravity.

On their way to the spot, they had swooped upon drug-stores, confiscated countless cartons of empty bottles. Now they ran into the clouding dust and were lost to view. As ambulances shrilled down the street, as radio patrol-cars flocked to the scene of mad confusion, the Intelligence operators carried out their strange orders....

Operator 5's swift roadster wormed its way through the swarm of fleeing cars. When Jimmy Christopher pulled the brake and leaped out, he peered with narrowed eyes at the widespread havoc. In a few moments, the newest, most modern skyscraper in the metropolis had been reduced to powdered stone and twisted steel, and now—

Out of the sky boomed mocking, gloating laughter—the laughter of the destroying god—just as the blood-red sun sank from sight....

WDC-13, CENTRAL headquarters of the United States Intelligence, consisted of a suite of windowless rooms shrewdly concealed from the workaday world of Washington, D.C. Its one secret entrance was carefully hidden and guarded. Its undercover force worked secretly, day and night, at the task of maintaining communication with sub-headquarters scattered over the whole world, at amplifying its gigantic files, at coördinating the innumerable activities of which the citizens it faithfully served never dreamed.

Tonight, an electrical tenseness strained the atmosphere in WDC-13. Numerous reports had flashed in over its secret web of wires, and from scattered points by means of radio. Desperate pleas came clicking over the teletypes:

OUR FORCE IS CRIPPLED... WE MUST HAVE MEN... SEND US MEN!

To which Z-7 could only respond:

NO MEN TO SEND... EVERY OFFICE IN THE COUNTRY HAS HEAVY LOSSES... EXECUTE ALL ORDERS REGARDLESS.

Frantic voices called on long-distance wires. "In God's name, what can we do? How can we protect ourselves? What is there to save us from being destroyed completely?" To which the dismay Z-7 could only answer: "I don't know! I don't know, and no man knows!"

But at that moment, working desperately in a laboratory hidden deep within the secret suite of WDC-13, Operator 5 was striving to learn that evil secret.

He had come by plane to Washington in response to the urgent orders of the Secretary of State. Tim Donovan and Diane Elliot had accompanied him while John Christopher had remained in New York to command the skull-headed band known as the Hidden Hundred. He had carried with him the strange phonograph records and a case of bottles brought to HN by puzzled Intelligence men from the wreckage of the International Broadcasting Corporation. Now, in the laboratory, while Tim Donovan anxiously watched, he undertook to analyze their contents.

His delay in reporting to the Secretary of State might, he realized, make his punishment even more drastic—but he chose the risk in the hope this analysis would be a clue to the secret of Kasma's power.

WITH THE utmost care, he discharged the contents of the bottles under water into special glassbells. Skillfully, he tested chemical reactions to reveal the nature of the gases they contained. Tim Donovan, watching, saw the same result follow the opening of each bottle. When, at last, Operator 5 abandoned the analysis, certain that each bottle was exactly the same, the boy asked anxiously:

"What have you found, Jimmy?"

"Nothing, Tim," Operator 5 answered in a whisper. "Absolutely nothing!"

"But those bottles—?"

"Contain only air." Jimmy Christopher, with a hopeless sigh, pulled off his chemist's smock. "A slight residue of stone dust from the destroyed building—a trace of carbon monoxide, normal in the city—but absolutely nothing suspicious. We've come to another dead end."

"Then the power of Kasma isn't electrical, and it isn't chemical?"

"Neither, Tim. That leaves a very narrow field of possibilities. The answer to the puzzle is in those phonograph records, I'm more convinced than ever. I'd hoped to be able to give the Secretary an enlightening report, Tim—but the mystery is increasingly baffling."

Operator 5 strode from the laboratory, into the office of Z-7. The chief knew at once, seeing Jimmy Christopher's expression of despair, that the analysis had been result-less. Diane Elliot came to Operator 5's side and he forced a wan smile.

"I'm still convinced that it is one thing—one force—that has all these varied effects. I'm certain there's absolutely nothing supernatural about it—that the explanation is a simple one. Yet now I'm absolutely at a loss. Chief, have you relayed my instructions?"

"Your instructions to investigate any suspicious preliminary activity in the buildings which were destroyed? Yes. But in the meantime—! These papers—just off the presses!"

Jimmy Christopher peered at startling black headlines:

MILLIONS FLOCKING TO WORSHIP OF KASMA!
SON OF KASMA DEMANDS FAITH; TERROR
SWEEPS NATION AS DESTRUCTION STRIKES!
GREAT LEADERS RENOUNCE CHRISTIANITY,
EMBRACE MYSTIC FAITH IN SELF-PRESERVA-
TION!
END OF WORLD PROMISED BY SON OF KASMA
UNLESS HIS FAITH IS ACCEPTED BY NATION!

HE TURNED slowly, strode out the door. Tim Donovan and Diane Elliot went with him, and the Washington chief followed to the secret elevator. They did not speak while they descended and passed through the guarded doors which concealed WDC-13 from the world. At the wheel of an Intelligence machine, Operator 5 drove rapidly toward the great building of the State, War and Navy Departments close by the White House.

Operator 5 and Z-7 entered the office of the Secretary of State, while Tim and the girl waited in the outer room. They faced the grim official across his desk. A moment of silence passed while the ranking member of the President's Cabinet, the commander of the vital governmental division which handles all international matters, faced Jimmy Christopher.

"I apologize for my delay, Mr. Secretary," Operator 5 said respectfully. "I confess that it is because I have persisted in disobeying your orders."

The Secretary rose stiffly. "Operator 5, I can no longer tolerate your insubordination. You have not only disobeyed orders, but you have neglected other, more important duties. I gave you special instructions to capture the leader of the Hidden Hundred. I ordered you to destroy that organization—and you have failed to do so. You leave me no choice."

Operator 5 leaned forward tensely. "Whatever action you take against me, Mr. Secretary, I cannot protest. You will be absolutely in the right—so far as regulations go. But before you punish me, I'd like to explain my reasons for violating and neglecting orders."

"Whatever you have to say," the Secretary returned frostily, "can have no affect whatever on my decision."

Grimly Operator 5 continued: "I violated and neglected orders, sir, so that I might serve a more vital cause. I am not in service to a set of hidebound rules. My oath is to protect and preserve my country. That duty always has been—always will be—uppermost in my mind and heart. Not your orders, nor those of any other man, sir, can keep me from fulfilling my pledge."

The Secretary's lips curled wryly.

"My violation of orders lies in my investigating the cult of Kasma. I warned before that it was a national menace, and you refuse to believe it. Now, sir, you cannot doubt that the country is rapidly passing under the control of a mystic alien. You cannot doubt that his weapon is terror, with which he intends to beat the people of the United States into abject slavery.

"We are not threatened with the power of a destroying god,

sir. We are the prey of the most gigantic plan to loot and ravish against the United States that ever was launched."

The Secretary remained silent.

"Perhaps you yourself heard the Son of Kasma speak to the people this afternoon. In plain words, he intends to wrest the control of this government from the hands of the leader to whom the people have given it. He asserted that the power of Kasma must reign supreme over the United States. He promised the very destruction I warned against—promised it as a blessing of Kasma!"

Still the Secretary remained silent.

"WE STILL have a chance to save the nation from domination by the Son of Kasma, from slavery under his Yellowese mystics—but our last chance is close at hand. Once that power is in his grasp, nothing can save us. We must expose him before he destroys this government. If we do not, we shall see our people made peons; we shall see the Son of Kasma reigning over our soil as a despotic monarch; we shall see our wealth confiscated by his band of ghastly fakers.

"We are not faced now merely with a strange power that wrecks single buildings and kills individual men, sir. We are faced with a far more dangerous force—the mass hysteria of a terrorized people."

"This nation," the Secretary drawled laconically, "is a democracy. The people's will is its very backbone. If it is this will we must combat now, we are faced with an absolutely hopeless task."

"Hopeless?" Operator 5 snapped. "Not, sir, in the minds of the very organization you have condemned—the Hidden

Hundred. You know that those men are serving their nation in their own way. Some of them have died in that service—and you condemn them as breakers of regulations! In these United States, Mr. Secretary, there are no truer patriots than the Hidden Hundred—and that, sir, is why I have failed to disband them."

The Secretary bristled. "You declare yourself in sympathy with that band of outlaws?"

"I do declare it, and proudly!" Operator 5 answered, his eyes blazing with deep lights. "Your orders have crippled the Intelligence—and the Hidden Hundred took up the tasks which became too great for the Service. Your orders broke those men, and yet they serve their nation faithfully. They are willing to die in dishonor, to starve, to hide like hunted animals, because of their patriotism. You may break me as you have broken them, Mr. Secretary—and I will be proud to continue to serve my nation exactly as they have served it."

The Secretary's face grew purple with wrath. "You dare—!"

"I dare tell you, sir, that nothing short of death or imprisonment will keep me from continuing to fight the power of Kasma, even after I am discharged from the Service. I promise you, Mr. Secretary, that to the best of my ability, as completely as I am able, I will see this case through to the end!"

The Secretary stiffened aghast. As he peered speechless at the cool face, at the determined eyes of Operator 5, Z-7 spoke huskily:

"Mr. Secretary, I plead with you to remember the exemplary service which Operator 5 has already rendered his country. He stands head and shoulders in ability, courage, and achievement over all my other men. There is no man I esteem more highly as an Intelligence operator or as a friend. I ask, respectfully, in this case, a special dispensation."

The Secretary snapped: *"What* do you ask?"

"Place Operator 5 strictly under my orders. Make him answerable to me, and to me only. In return, I will accept the complete responsibility for his acts."

"You are an unwise man, Z-7," the Secretary declared, "to make yourself liable for the disastrous foolhardiness of this young man."

THE CHIEF declared warmly: "You may consider me fully responsible for him, in every way. I make this offer, sir, so that Operator 5 may continue in the Service. The Intelligence is my whole life—if I lose it, I have nothing. Yet I would rather step out of the Service at this minute than see Operator 5 dismissed."

The Secretary straightened, studying the haggard face of Z-7. Operator 5's dark eyes glowed at the chief. His heart warmed at this complete expression of personal faith and esteem. He could say nothing while Z-7 withstood the stern stare of the Secretary.

"You make this offer even though you realize that some rash act of Operator 5 may result in *your* being dismissed too, Z-7?"

"I do."

The Secretary peered at Operator 5. "I cannot refuse Z-7's appeal. Yet I must warn you again, Operator 5—warn you that now you face not only your own dishonor, but also that of the chief of the Intelligence. You might choose to risk your own standing in the Service—but you simply cannot risk the honor of your chief."

Operator 5 said quietly: "I realize the fullness of the faith that Z-7 places in me, Mr. Secretary. I shall never forget it."

"Very well. This, Operator 5, is your last chance as long as I am commander-in-chief of the Intelligence. If you force me to break Z-7, I shall not spare you from the worst punishment it is possible for me to pronounce!"

In a whisper, Operator 5 murmured: "Thank you, chief—from the bottom of my heart!"

They were startled by the sudden opening of a door. The man who strode into the room was an Assistant Secretary in the State Department. His face was white; his eyes were widened, and as he came to a stop at his superior's desk, his lips worked wordlessly.

"Sir, you know that Congress is in session tonight—that both houses are in extraordinary meeting now, considering the allotment of the latest appropriation bills."

"Yes, yes!" the Secretary snapped. "What of it, Gregory? Speak up, man!"

"Something—something strange—is happening there tonight, sir! The federal matters before Congress have been forgotten. I've just come from the gallery, sir. They are talking of nothing except the power of Kasma."

"What? Are they crazy?"

"I've never seen anything like this before, sir," the Assistant Secretary gasped. "It is a thing which would have been shouted down in derision at any other time—but not now. They are listening spellbound to Senator Hodkin. *He* may be mad, sir, but if he is—they all are! It's as though they are all hypnotized—all under the power of this strange god, for—"

Z-7 snapped "In God's name, what's happening there? Out with it!"

"Hodkin is urging the passage of a resolution renouncing Christianity, declaring Kasma to be the true faith! He is urging Congress to expend all current appropriations in erecting temples to Kasma, on building a national organization for the new religion. That measure will be passed, sir—I promise you it will be passed—and it means rifling our treasury for the benefit of mystic aliens!"

Operator 5 turned sharply, his eyes shining with alarm. "Mr. Secretary, I urge you to go to the Capitol at once—to see for yourself the power of Kasma working to loot this nation!"

CHAPTER 8
SLAVE OF THE POWER

THE INTELLIGENCE car sped to the base of the broad steps of the national Capitol. Operator 5 was first out of it. Tim Donovan and Diane Elliot came to his sides as Z-7 and the Secretary of State alighted. In their pressing anxiety, they did not speak as they ran up the wide stone flight, across the portico of the famed building, toward the gallery of the Hall of Representatives.

Abruptly they paused as they neared the door. They stood stock-still, peering at each other strangely. Mystification shone in the eyes of the Secretary and Z-7 and Diane Elliot; dismay drew deep lines in the faces of Operator 5 and Tim Donovan. The uncanny apathy which seized them was being felt for the first time by the two officials and the girl, but Jimmy Christopher and the boy recognized the dread effects instantly.

Here, within the historic walls of the Capitol, the hypnotic power of Kasma was weaving its evil spell!

Operator 5 started away, exerting all his strength against the narcotic stupor. The Secretary and Z-7 forced themselves to follow, and the girl came after them as if walking in a strange dream-world. They passed slowly along the gallery, gazed down into the great Hall of Representatives, where both houses of Congress had met in extraordinary session.

The man who was shouting zealously at his colleagues, was Senator Hodkin—a man whom Operator 5 had seen kneeling before the power of Kasma in the hidden temple in New York!

"We can recognize no authority now save the power of the god that is destroying the world of the unfaithful! We owe no allegiance higher than our duty to him. Unless we pledge ourselves to his faith, we are doomed! I plead with this Congress to pass these measures as a small tribute to the power of Kasma!"

A hush filled the hall as the Senator finished. Solemnly, the Speaker of the House rose and rapped his gavel. His grave tones ordered a vote upon the appropriation measures, and immediately the roll call was begun. Operator 5 watched from the gallery as name after name was called, as the votes were recorded.

"Aye..! Aye..! Aye..! Aye..!"

Z-7 passed a trembling hand across his pale face and muttered: "God! The measures will pass without a dissenting vote! It means that our government will be bled white while these great appropriations will be spent in the cause of Kasma!"

The Secretary of State mumbled in a low tone: "It means the complete disruption of the federal government—it means making Kasma the all-powerful ruler of the country!"

The voting continued in awed monotone as members of the Congress responded to the calling of their names: "Aye..! Aye..! Aye..!"

Operator 5 whispered: "But this is only the first step. These measures are being passed and will be passed again, over-whelmingly, if the President vetoes them. We will see this scene repeated, and each time it will lift the Son of Kasma higher in power until he reigns as the absolute monarch over what was once the United States!"

THE SECRETARY OF STATE turned slowly away, forced himself through the door of the gallery. Operator 5 touched Diane Elliot's arm. The girl turned, dazed, as if she scarcely heard Jimmy Christopher.

"Follow him, Di! Watch him! The chief and I will be along to take your place as soon as we have talked with the President about his calamity.... Hurry, Di!"

The girl made a visible effort to steady herself, to combat the evil stupor that was upon her. She took the keys of the Intel-ligence car which Operator 5 proffered her, forced herself out the door after the Secretary. Jimmy Christopher, Z-7 and Tim Donovan waited in the gallery, listening to the monotonously repeated vote of "Aye!" as the girl followed orders.

Once she reached the entrance of the Capitol, she felt the

weird hypnotic effects pass. In a moment she was again in complete possession of her senses. Now alert, though puzzled by the lethargy that had seized her, she ran down the steps. She reached the Secretary's side and exclaimed: "I'll drive you back to your office, sir!"

Speechless with dismay, the Secretary settled in the car while the girl took the wheel. She drove quickly and neither of them spoke. Profound consternation silenced them. When the girl drew the car to a stop at the front of the huge State, War and Navy Building, the Secretary mumbled his thanks and stepped out. Diane followed quickly. And again, suddenly, appallingly, they felt the numbing effects of the spell of Kasma!

A figure glided out of the darkness, a being that appeared to be a scarlet ghost with yellow face. It came from shadows without sound, stood before them, peering with gleaming, black, slanted eyes. Capacity for feeling, for thinking, passed beyond them as they confronted the Son of Kasma.

The yellow lips parted and a single command issued: "Follow!"

While the eyes of the Son of Kasma gripped them, they took a few, short, heavy steps toward a gleaming black sedan waiting beside a black truck. Inside the passenger car, two black-robed Yellowese were waiting. The door opened in silent invitation. Diane Elliot entered it first, unable to control her own volition; and the Secretary followed. The door slammed shut, and a motor whirred.

In the main office of the Department of State, Assistant Secretary Gregory had been pacing anxiously. He paused to peer out the window. The sight he saw stunned him, held him spellbound with incredulous wonder. He saw the door of a huge black sedan closing upon the Secretary, a blood-red figure gliding through the gloom. He peered transfixed at the Son of Kasma.

A gasp broke from his lips as he whirled to the telephone. He blurted the secret number of WDC-13. Over the line his dismayed cry carried:

"The Son of Kasma has taken the Secretary prisoner!"

Z-7'S HEELS beat across the floor of his office in WDC-13. His face was graven deep with lines of worry; his dark eyes smoldered with fury. Operator 5 stood quietly beside the desk as long, torturous minutes ticked past.

They had rushed to the central headquarters after hearing that the Secretary of State had been spirited away by the Son of Kasma. Z-7 had immediately issued orders marshaling the entire Intelligence force in Washington into a desperate manhunt for the important Cabinet member. For hours the search had been under way while all other duties of the Service remained in suspension. Now, slowly, reports from the searchers began to click into the communications-room.

" 'Not found!'" Z-7 snapped. "Over and over again, the same thing—'not found'! Not many more men to be heard from—and absolutely no result!"

Operator 5 had been swiftly reading those reports Z-7 had tossed aside unread. His mind worked at high speed as he noted a response to his orders for investigation of preliminaries to the destruction of buildings which the power of Kasma had razed.

The information he had now quickened his heart with a hope that at last a clue had come to hand:

> ... WDC-13... ANSWERING SPECIAL ORDERS 45791... HAVE DISCOVERED POSSIBLE PREPARATIONS FOR DESTRUCTION OF BUILDINGS WRECKED BY STRANGE POWER... SAME PROCEDURE IN EACH CASE... MEN FROM U.S. COAST AND GEODETIC SURVEY CAME TO BUILDINGS WEEKS AGO PURPORTING TO MAKE VIBRATION TESTS... SMALL MACHINE WITH THREE UNBALANCED WHEELS PLACED IN BASEMENTS BRACED BY BEAMS AGAINST THE WALLS... MACHINE SENT VIBRATIONS OF VARYING FREQUENCY THROUGH WALLS... RECORDING INSTRUMENTS PLACED ON UPPER FLOORS DETECTED FREQUENCY AT WHICH BUILDING VIBRATED... VIBRATIONS INFINITESIMAL BUT NATURAL RESONANCE PITCH OF BUILDINGS WAS FOUND... TESTS WERE NOT AUTHORIZED BY GOVERNMENT... EXPERTS IMPOSTERS... TESTS MADE ON ALL DESTROYED BUILDINGS AND FOLLOWING: SUB-TREASURY STOCK EXCHANGE IN NEW YORK CITY... CHURCHES IN CHICAGO, NEW ORLEANS, ST. LOUIS, DENVER, SEATTLE, LOS ANGELES....

" 'Not found!'" Z-7 exploded so violently that Operator 5 was startled. "The last report has come in!" The Washington chief was staring at a scrawled flimsy. "Our last man reports failure! We have not been able to find the Secretary and Diane!"

JIMMY CHRISTOPHER glanced quickly at another report which he had taken from Z-7's desk.

> … WDC4J… REPORT INVESTIGATION TEMPLE FIRE NEW YORK… VARIED ELECTRICAL EQUIP-MENT DESTROYED ON UPPER FLOORS… MOST REMARKABLE ITEM HUGE COIL APPARENTLY POWERFUL ELECTROMAGNET… CORE THICK AS MAN'S BODY WOUND WITH MILES OF COPPER WIRE… POSSIBLE USE UNKNOWN….

"In God's name, what can we do?" Z-7 moaned as he sank into his chair. "We're helpless before the power of Kasma. We have scarcely any force left to fight it. Hour by hour, the service is growing weaker while the power of Kasma strengthens. It's impossible to cope with that force!"

Still another report from the New York headquarters drew Operator 5's attention:

> … WDC-13… BROADCAST BY SON OF KASMA PRE-ARRANGED… MICROPHONES IN NEARBY OFFICE BUILDING TO MAIN LINE FROM STUDIO TO LONG ISLAND ANTENNA… SON OF KASMA THUS ABLE TO SPEAK OVER NATION-WIDE NETWORK… TEMPORARY STUDIO THEN ABAN-DONED… SIGNIFIES DEEP-LAID PLAN PREPARED IN ADVANCE… HN….

Operator 5 declared quietly: "I still believe it's not impossible to fight Kasma's power, Chief. I'm not through yet by any means. I think I have a lead which may explain what this diabolical force is, and—"

"But it's not that destructive force which concerns us most now!" Z-7 protested. "It's the terror of our people—the overpowering momentum of a hundred and twenty million souls flocking to worship Kasma. That—that is a force which we cannot hope to combat!"

"Chief, I'm going straight ahead!"

Z-7's black eyes smoldered. "I need not remind you that you're under my orders. I refuse to let you throw your life away—no matter what risks you want to take! Listen to me, Operator 5. I am giving you orders!"

Tightly, Jimmy Christopher asked: "Yes, Chief?"

"Abandon this case at once!"

Operator 5 stood motionless, his dark blue eyes shining brilliantly. His lips pressed hard, and he spoke no word. His face went white as his jaws clamped. Then, abruptly, he turned from Z-7. He thrust out the door of the inner—office and slammed it hard behind him.

Z-7 peered after him grimly. The chief's finger quickly touched a button on his desk. Immediately another door opened and two Intelligence operators entered. They were two of the most capable undercover agents in the service: they had just returned from a wearing, fruitless search for the Secretary of State. F-6 and V-9 heard Z-7's voice crackle grimly:

"Follow Operator 5! Watch him constantly! I have ordered

him off this case. If he persists, you are to place him under arrest and hold him prisoner!"

F-6 and V-9 hurried from the inner office. They found the corridor empty, the panel of the secret elevator closed. Jimmy Christopher was already hastening from WDC-13. As the two grim agents reached the street, they glimpsed Operator 5's roadster traveling rapidly up the avenue. They sped to a waiting Intelligence machine, sent it careening in the same direction. Jimmy Christopher, hands wrapped white on the wheel of his powerful car, was unaware that he was being trailed by two grim comrades.

He sped toward the White House....

THE SECRET SERVICE men stationed at the gate of the White House passed Operator 5's car at a glance. When he entered the East Wing of the historic mansion, the President's secretary hurried to him. In answer to his urgent request, the secretary said: "But the President can not be disturbed now. He is talking with the Vice-President. He is aware—"

Jimmy Christopher stepped past, strode directly to the door of the President's study. He ignored the protesting Secret Service agent stationed there, stepped through into the room where the President handled the executive duties of the nation. He came to a stop, said quickly, respectfully:

"I beg your pardon, gentlemen, but a matter of the utmost urgency forces this interruption."

The President's kindly face was grave, his eyes worried. The man who stood beside him was white-haired, stocky, a politician of the old school—the Vice-President of the United States. They both gripped Operator 5's hand when he came to the desk. The President said slowly:

"I'm glad you've come, Operator 5. A strange thing has just happened. The Vice- President has come here in response to a message which I did not send!"

Jimmy Christopher's eyes widened as he looked at the sheet of official stationery which the Chief Executive handed him. It was a penciled request for the Vice-President to call at the White House at this hour. It bore a signature which appeared to be the President's.

"A forgery!"

The Vice-President muttered: "But what can it mean?"

Operator 5 answered quickly: "You have been brought together here for a reason. There can only be one! Both of you are marked for victims of Kasma's power!"

The President stared. The Vice-President sank into his chair in dismay. Operator 5 leaned forward tensely:

"Anything is possible for Kasma—and we must be prepared! This forged note, gentlemen, can mean only that the Son of Kasma is already moving to seize control of the whole government!

"Moreover, he intends to act tonight—within a few minutes— while that forged note keeps you together in this room!"

The Vice-President stared, exclaimed: "What the devil do you mean?"

Swiftly Operator 5 explained. "The Secretary of State is now the prisoner of the cult of mystics. Picture him as under that deadly influence; his mind merely a passive instrument to obey as Kasma commands. If, gentlemen, you should both be assassinated tonight, the Secretary of State will reappear. He will be unable to think, to act, except as the Son of Kasma directs him. He will not veto the vast appropriations bill—voted to Kasma tonight by an enslaved Congress—as you will. Through him, the Son of Kasma will become the absolute monarch—the pillager of this nation!"

The President blurted: "The Son of Kasma—reach us here? How is it possible? No one can get at us. We cannot be touched—"

"No guards can stop Kasma. These walls can't hold his power back. At any moment, it may strike—and kill you on the spot. You've got to leave the White House, gentlemen, at once—and secretly."

THE PRESIDENT repeated: " 'Secretly?' The White House detail of the Secret Service cannot leave my side. There is no way of secretly—"

"You must trust me, sir! Unless you make this move—unless you both are willing to be hidden and to remain hidden—nothing can save you and this nation from doom!"

The President's hand moved to a button on his desk. Then he strode to the door. Across the sill he faced the Secret Service agent to whom was entrusted the duty of protecting the Chief Executive—a man whose constant vigilance was ordained by a law which even the President could not set aside.

"Call all the men of your detail together in the Green Room at once," the President directed. "We're faced with the necessity of taking extraordinary precautions. All your men, understand? The meeting will be short, and I will join you in a moment."

"Yes, sir."

The President closed the door, listened to the sounds which meant that the Secret Service agents were being summoned from their posts. Quickly he gestured Operator 5 and the Vice-President through a door at the side of the study. They passed quickly through a series of rooms into the hallway near the East Wing entrance. There, the two executives again listened.

The men are in the Green Room now. We must hurry or they'll suspect a trick. Operator 5—we're waiting for instructions."

"Follow me, gentlemen—quickly!"

Jimmy Christopher stepped into the hallway. It was empty. Looking out the entrance, he saw that, for the moment, the way out was open. At his gesture, the President and the Vice-President followed him. As they crossed the sill, a gasp of dismay broke from Jimmy Christopher's lips.

A leaden feeling enveloped him; a numbness pervaded his mind…!

"It's beginning to act now! The power! Get into the car! Fight it; move as quickly as you can!"

The two dismayed men hesitated a moment, stunned by the weird lethargy that crept upon them. Operator 5 seized their arms, hurried them toward his waiting roadster. As the President and Vice-President entered it, the appalling numbness grew stronger. Jimmy Christopher, forcing himself to desperate action, began to climb to the wheel; but he paused in dismay.

Two men were moving toward him through the shadows—moving like creatures in a dream. He recognized their drawn faces. They were F-6 and V-9, the agents ordered by Z-7 to trail Operator 5 to keep him from further work on the case.

F-6 gasped: "Hold on there! In God's name, you can't take—!"

"You're under arrest, Operator 5!" V-9 blurted huskily.

Jimmy Christopher summoned all his strength as he whirled at them. "Orders of Z-7!" broke from the numb lips of F-6 at the very moment when Operator 5 struck. His smashing blow drove the undercover man backward. He drove out his fist again, full between V-9's eyes.

Desperately he climbed to the wheel. Each movement a strain, each moment an eternity, he forced himself to throw the car into gear and start it off.

The roadster turned into the street. Suddenly the hypnotic effect of the spell of Kasma began to lessen. Desperately heartened, Operator 5 sent the car speeding—and the apathy vanished from his mind and body. At top speed, he sent the roadster whizzing along the dark street....

CHAPTER 9
THE SECRET OF KASMA

IN COLD fury, Z-7 paced the inner office of WDC-13. He was still stunned by the amazing message that had flashed to him from the White House. Again he ordered all his force of operators in Washington into a frantic search—this time for the President, the Vice-President, and Operator 5. Reports hashed to his desk one after another, each carrying the same dread message. The search was fruitless.

The long hours had strained Z-7's nerves. His face was haggard; his eyes smoldered; his heart was a thing that pounded dully, heavily. Exhaustion had nearly conquered him when he was startled by the sudden opening of the communications-room door. The chief-dispatcher gazed in wide-eyed and blurted:

"Chief, Operator 5 is coming into headquarters now!"

At that moment, the outer door opened. Jimmy Christopher stepped into the office. His face was grave, his lips hard-pressed as he paused, facing Z-7. His eyes glittered with determined brightness; and for a moment no word was spoken.

Z-7 demanded at last: "Operator 5, is it true that you are responsible for the disappearance of the President and the Vice-President from the White House?"

"It is, Chief."

"Then where are they? I have had all my men searching for them for hours. *Where are they?*"

"I can't reveal where the President and Vice-President are, Chief, even to you."

Z-7 stood stunned, motionless, while Operator 5 turned sharply. Tim Donovan followed Jimmy Christopher out of the inner office and along a hallway. They entered a door together, and Z-7 followed in time to see it close. He strode to it heavily, grasped the knob—and found it locked.

"Open this door!"

Through the panels. Operator 5 spoke quietly. "Chief, please trust me. I have a lot of work to do, and I must do it alone—now."

Z-7 blurted: "You're mad!"

Operator 5's reply was a question. "Have you a report from the White House, Chief?"

THE CHIEF'S shoulders sagged. "Yes—?"

"Two men of the White House Secret Service detail went into the President's study and found him missing. A moment later, they were found there—dead."

"Killed by the power of Kasma, Chief! Thank God it was not the President and the Vice-President who were found there! They are safe now. They must remain hidden until all danger is past. The nation must not know they are missing. Regardless of anything else, Chief, you must see to that."

Z-7 declared huskily: "Operator 5, I don't know what to say. If when the Secretary of State returns, this will mean the end of both of us in the service. I placed my trust in you—because I could not dream that you would do a thing like this to me."

"I know, Chief." Operator 5's answer was almost inaudible. "Please believe that I have only done my best. But not even your trust in me, not even your place in this service, can stand before my pledge to my country."

Jimmy Christopher turned slowly from the door. His movements became brisk as he passed to other doors and made sure they were bolted. Tim Donovan followed his moves in dismay and wonder. Operator 5 paused, eyes narrowed in thought, in the center of the suite of rooms which comprised the WDC-13 laboratory.

Tim Donovan stood by silently while Jimmy Christopher stripped off coat and vest and rolled his sleeves. To these rooms, he had brought the dozen mysterious phonographs found in the Temple of Kasma. He carried them to a bench where two turntables sat—apparatus used at times for the transcribing of intercepted telephone conversations made originally on wax-cylinders. Operator 5 started the needle in the groove of one—and no sound emerged from the horn....

"Jimmy." Tim Donovan spoke quietly. "You're letting it get you. Maybe if you made a fresh start, it will work out. Get your mind off it for a few minutes, and try again."

Operator 5 sighed, "Maybe you're right, Tim."

The boy grinned. "Sure. When you showed me those two tricks at home, you didn't have a chance to tell me how to do them. Show me now."

Jimmy Christopher's lips reflected the boy's smile. "Okay, Tim. You know what you're doing, don't you? You hope that my concentrating on something else for a while will give me a new slant on the puzzle of Kasma's power. Let's try it."

OPERATOR 5 went to a desk in the corner of the lab, and found a pack of cards in a drawer. He selected all the kings and queens from it while Tim waited eagerly.

"Remember the first trick? I showed you these kings and queens; then you cut the packet repeatedly. I took them from behind my back two at a time, and each time it was the king and queen of the same suit. Next you cut them again, and the last time I was able to separate all the kings from all the queens. Simplest thing in the world, Tim.

143

"When you begin, you hold the eight cards together. From left to right come the four kings, then the four queens. Notice, though, Tim, that the sequence of suits of the kings and queens is exactly the same. That is, the first card on the left as I fan them and show them to you now is the king of hearts; the second is the king of clubs; the third is the king of diamonds; the fourth is the king of spades. Then comes the queen of hearts, then clubs, then diamonds, then spades, in the same order. Once you've made that simple preparation, the trick's all set."

"Gee, is that all, Jimmy?"

"Almost, Tim. Your cutting the packet of eight cards made no difference whatever in the final result. Now watch. Holding the cards behind my back, I separate the top four cards from the bottom four. I hold them in my left hand, and with the right I draw off the top card of each group. There you are—a king and queen of the same suit. It works automatically all the way through."

"Doggone!" Tim blurted.

"Now we gather the cards for the second effect. In doing that, be sure the king is below the queen in each pair. Again, cutting the packet of eight doesn't make any difference in the end. Now, watch again.

"I hold the eight cards in my left hand behind my back. I draw off the top one between the thumb and forefinger of my right hand, then the second one between the first and second fingers, then the third between the thumb and forefinger again, and so on. In other words, each alternate card is grouped, four in each.

And there are, the kings all together in one and the queens all together in the other."

"Gee, Jimmy, that's slick—and it's easy to do, too!" The boy's eyes lighted with delight. "It's all clear all of a sudden, and you're going to get at the secret of Kasma's power in just the same way."

"I hope so, Tim," Operator 5 said gravely. "Now I'll explain the second trick, the card circle. Remember it? I gave you the pack, and you cut it and lifted a few cards out of the middle. You counted those you took and noted the card on the bottom. I then dealt twenty or so cards out on the table in a spiral. The card I picked showed the number you had selected. Next you named your card, after I'd picked up another, and the card in my hand turned out to be the one you named. It's very simple, too, Tim.

"You prepare the deck by taking thirteen cards, from a king down to an ace—the suits don't matter—and put them on the top of the deck. Then you're all set.

"Now we begin. The deck is cut. The spectator takes his packet from the *lower* half of the cut deck. After he notes the number of cards and the bottom card in the packet, he places the packet on top of the *upper* part of the deck. Now you deal the spiral of cards, face down, of course. All you do now is count to the fourteenth card in the circle.

"That one automatically indicates the number of cards chosen by the spectator—always. What's more, it tells you the location of the spectator's card. A six, for instance, tells you there were six cards in his packet. Therefore his card is the sixth you dealt. You spot it, then move all the cards about confusedly, but you don't lose sight of it, of course. Then you pick it up, ask him to name his card—and you already have it! That's all—"

Operator 5 paused abruptly, his eyes suddenly shining and lifted. He blurted: "That's it! That's it, of course!"

TIM GAZED at him amazed as he turned again to the electric turntables. With feverish haste, he unbolted and removed the amplifying unit. It was a resistor-coupler device of high power. Operator 5 tore the resistors from their clips, selected others from a box in the electrical bench, and clipped them into place. He also replaced the coupling condensers with others of lesser strength. Then again he started both records playing on the two turntables, and stood back, listening intently.

"I've raised the response level, Tim, that's all," he whispered. "It was adjusted to reproduce voices perfectly, but sounds of higher frequency—yes!"

A strange rhythm was beating through the air. It was a regular series of impulses that made a treble hum. Operator 5 eagerly lifted the needle from one of the records, and the sound stopped. It returned when both records were playing together, but vanished when he raised the pick-up from either. He stepped back with an exclamation of elation.

"Yes, that's it! What you're hearing, Tim, is a sound that is not actually recorded on either record. The sounds on both records is so high in pitch that your ear can't hear them. But when both play together, there is a discord beat—the hum you're hearing—a heterodyne note.* We're getting at it!"

Again, quickly, he tore the resistors and condensers from their clips and substituted others which would make the amplifier capable of reproducing sounds of extremely high frequency. At his next attempt, the heterodyne note was stronger. He shut off the machine, and hurried eagerly into the library adjoining the lab. There Tim Donovan watched him probe into the vast files, then jerk volume after volume off the shelves and examine certain pages thoroughly.

Mystified, the boy followed when Jimmy Christopher returned to the lab. He made further preparations which Tim could not understand. At last, anxiously, he strode to the main entrance, and unbolted it. His voice rang clearly: "Chief!"

Z-7's slow steps came down the corridor. His haggard eyes turned gravely toward Operator 5. Jimmy Christopher, in his intense elation, seized Z-7's arm and hurried him forward.

"I think I've got it, Chief!"

"What?"

"I may be wrong—but I feel it's the answer. Stand right here, Chief—facing the phonograph. I've made certain adjustments.

---

* Author's Note: When two frequencies are superimposed, they fall into step at regular intervals, producing a beat called the heterodyne. This principle is made use of in radio in the design of the superheterodyne receiver. In physical research, the heterodyne beat is used to determine the frequency of unknown impulses.

I'm going to play one of these records, simply that and nothing more. I want you to tell me if you feel anything unusual."

Z-7 watched curiously as the test began. Operator 5 turned the volume control of the reproducer full on while the chief faced it. The needle began tracing the red grooves. For a moment there was no breath taken in that laboratory. Z-7's eyes widened with dismay.

"I—I'm feeling the same apathy that I felt in the Capitol! The same sensation—though it's so faint I'm hardly sure of it!"

"That's it, chief! If this amplified were thousands of times more powerful, you would be overcome by exactly the effect. This is the secret we've been looking for. The power of Kasma is not an electrical or chemical force—it's a physical power—*sound!*"

"Sound?" Z-7 repeated. "But I heard nothing!"

JIMMY CHRISTOPHER placed on the desk the volumes he had brought from the library. "Chief, let me explain carefully. Sound travels in waves. These waves create pressure. Powerful noises have a strong, physical effect. A common example is the shell-shock suffered during the World War. You know how you wince with pain even when a radio is turned on full blast. Here, Chief, is an item from the files concerning a gigantic loud-speaker which is able to magnify the human voice a million times."*

Z-7 glanced at the printed article as Operator 5 raced on.

---

* AUTHOR'S NOTE: This huge loudspeaker, built by the Western Electric Company, was used for the first time during the recent international yacht races. Its horn, of cast aluminum, can magnify the human voice until it is a

"It can project human speech over a distance of miles. Here is a phrase to be noted carefully, chief. 'At full power, the device hurls sound into the air with a force of a fifty-pound sledgehammer.' There is a newspaper clipping. Chief, telling of the physical effects of the speaker when it was used experimentally in the open. 'Men were stunned, a boy was knocked unconscious, and birds dropped dead from the air as the terrific burst of sound struck them!'"

"But what connection has this?" Z-7 demanded. "When the buildings collapsed, when Kasma's victims dropped dead, there was no blast of sound to do it."

"Exactly!" Operator 5 indicated another heavy tone. "No sound that could be heard—but an inaudible sound was there. The eye is sensitive to only a small section of the vibration waveband, you know. We can't see ultra-violet light, heat-waves, or radio impulses, but they are akin to the light we do see. In the same way, there are ranges of sound which the human ear cannot hear."

"But sound alone could not—"

"Wait, Chief. It all links together in the end—you'll soon see it. There is a phenomenon in sound physics known as resonance. Imagine two violins in perfect pitch. The G string of one is strummed. The G string of the other gives off a note, though it is not touched. That is because it is in resonance. The impulses of the first vibrating string strike the second and it vibrates in

roar 1,000 times louder than the roar at the foot of Niagara Falls. Operator 5's further statements, made here concerning it, are fact.

unison. Everything, Chief—everything—has a certain point of resonance of its own to which it will respond.

"Take a familiar example. Army officers, leading a company of soldiers across a bridge, order them to break step. If they did not, the rhythmic tread of the marching feet might fall into tune with the natural resonance of the span. It would set up powerful vibrations which each step in unison would make more powerful—and if it persisted, that bridge would collapse."

"Yes—that's true!"

THIS PRINCIPAL of resonance is one of the miracles of physics. Suppose a steel I-beam is supported at both ends. That beam has a certain pitch of resonance. Suppose we know what that frequency is—the number of impulses per second which will make the beam respond in natural vibration. Suppose we begin gently striking the beam exactly that number of times per second. The beam will immediately respond. Each vibration will grow stronger than the last, each new impulse will exert greater force. It is absolutely true, Chief, that the beam can be caused to burst into bits with the violence of the vibrations brought into it merely by drops of water regularly striking it!"

Z-7 stared.

"Buildings also have their resonance point. Earthquakes are vibrations. After some earthquakes, it has been observed that tall buildings withstood the shock while smaller ones went to pieces. That isn't because the tall ones were better constructed—the reverse might be true. It's because the earthquake struck the natural resonance point of the small buildings, and not that of the taller.

"The U.S. Coast and Geodetic Survey has been using a machine in the West Coast cities to test the vulnerability of buildings to earthquake shocks. It is a small device no bigger than a grindstone, but when it is operating it can make the tallest structure respond to its vibration. That vibration point is found by changing the speed of the eccentric wheels of the device. To these experts, Chief, it is an everyday job to make great skyscrapers tremble slightly by adjusting the speed of the wheels to the proper point. And a machine of that sort paved the way for the power of Kasma to strike!"

Z-7 was listening intently.

"Buildings, according to their size, have resonance pitches below the limits of sensitivity of the human ear in sound. But if impulses of the correct frequency are directed at a building, and if they persist, the violence of the vibrations will in the end become so great that that building will fall to pieces!"

"By God, you've got it!" Z-7 blurted. "But that's only part of the power—"

"Listen, Chief! Here are reports on special researches into the physical effects of sounds, including sounds which the human ear can't hear. For instance, Professor Harold Burris-Meyer, of Stevens Institute of Technology, has experimented with inaudible sounds to produce atmospheric effects for theater presentations. Read this—and it is only a hint of what is possible."

Operator 5 pointed to:

"A series of grating noises, totally unheard, can make one feel as though his teeth—were chattering, or can even make one break out in perspiration for no obvious reason.

"With the control of sounds, cold or warm moods can be created in an audience. All of the symptoms of fear or joy can be attained by the sheer use of different pitches of sound. So great is this power that a theatre balcony can be made to jump up and down." *

"And this, Chief!"

Hysteria can be induced in an audience in less than forty seconds by sound treatment.

"We have been able to stimulate physiological reactions so violent as to be definitely pathological," Professor Burris-Meyer declared." **

"And to go even farther, Chief," Operator 5 declared breathlessly, "read this further report by Hiram Percy Maxim, the great inventor:"

… To lead the vibrations to the point at which they are wanted, the crystal is immersed in oil. A small glass tube, dipping into this oil, will carry the vibrations to the desired spot.

When squeezed between the fingers, the glass tube will "burn" the skin. In a few minutes it would cut through the fingers. It will also eat into wood, even drill a hole in glass, spouting out

---

* AUTHOR'S NOTE: Statements made by Professor Burris-Meyer before the National Theatre Conference in New Haven, Conn., on Feb. 23, 1935.
** AUTHOR'S NOTE: Statements made by Professor Burris-Meyer before the meeting of the Acoustical Society of America, in New York City, soon after the above.

pulverized glass having the fineness of steam.

Water set into vibration is sterilized. Small fish, reptiles and vegetable matter are instantly killed.

"The power of Kasma to murder, Chief! And this other note!"

The air ordinarily present in water is driven out, making it fizz like soda-water.*

"That's the secret of Kasma's rain-making! Certain frequencies sent through the air cause the moisture held in it to condense. Invisible sound created the deluges of rain!"

Z-7's black eyes smoldered as he peered at Operator 5's eager face.

"There is only one more point to be explained, Chief—the way these predatory mystics have applied this force of inaudible sound. That is not difficult. The great iron coil, the huge magnet, found in the ruins of the burned temple, give the answer. That is the remains of a gigantic loudspeaker, huger than the one built by the Western Electric Company. It shot out tremendously powerful beams of vibrations. They originated on these phonograph records, were amplified millions of times, and exerted their terrible effects, though the ear could not hear them!"

Z-7 exclaimed: "You're right! You must be right!"

"**WHEN I** trailed the Son of Kasma's car up Riverside Drive Chief, a covered truck traveled with it. Now we know why. There was a huge loudspeaker in that truck. The rear of it was probably

---

* AUTHOR'S NOTE: From a report by Hiram Percy Maxim published in New York late in April, 1935.

thin cloth painted to look like metal. Through it came a powerful blast of inaudible sound. The vibration was one selected for the purpose—to stun anyone who followed.

"In that same way, our Intelligence force has been crippled. Every one of our men who has been killed, who has gone mad, who has suffered the loss of his memory, is the victim of a sound-beam issuing from a concealed, portable loudspeaker of great power."

"But—it must be a terrifically powerful beam which can crush a great building down!" Z-7 interposed.

Operator 5's eyes blazed. "There is only one answer to that, Chief. Not only is it the most powerful amplifying unit and the hugest loudspeaker in the world, that destroyed the buildings, but it is mobile. It struck at the Mexican border, next in New York, then in Philadelphia. It turned its effects on the *Bethlehem* at sea, again upon New York, then upon Washington. There cannot be more than one of these gigantic devices—therefore that one can be transported quickly, and its beam directed on the doomed spot.

"That force, Chief, struck from the sky!"

"What?"

"There is no other answer. The source of these destructive, unhearable beams of sound floats in the air—some kind of a dirigible. Picture it, Chief! This craft, high in the sky, turns its invisible and silent power downward. According to the frequency it blasts out, rain may fall. By choosing the frequency of the building marked for doom—one already determined by vibrator-machine test—that building is made to crash. There,

Chief, is the answer to the secret of the power of Kasma—and even as we learn of it, it may be striking again."

Z-7 straightened grimly, about to speak.

"Chief, you've put me under arrest." Operator 5 went on hastily. "I do not blame you for that—but I beg of you, let me go ahead with this case. Let me see it through to the finish. We may be helpless to save ourselves from the devilish cult of Kasma now—but let me try!"

Z-7 smiled, a glint of fighting spirit in his black eyes: "Go to it, Operator 5, and more power to you!"

Operator 5 exclaimed: "Thanks, Chief! We must be prepared for the next time Kasma strikes. In this report, there is mention of other buildings which have been pre-tested for resonance. The most important among them are the Sub-Treasury and the Stock Exchange building in New York City. They're nearby each other on Wall Street. Chief, I want to be prepared to seek out the source of Kasma's power if the blow falls upon either of those buildings. Will you relay my orders?"

"I will!"

Z-7 came stiffly to his feet, his jaw-muscles bunched, his black eyes smouldering, gripped Jimmy Christopher's hand.

"Our last chance, Chief," Operator 5 declared grimly. "Our last!"

CHAPTER 10
SKY MONSTER SIGHTED

IN A black room, hidden far from the humming hub of the nation's capitol, two men sat silent. Their faces were anxious, their eyes filled with dread. They had spent long hours here, behind locked doors, virtual prisoners. The President and the Vice-President of the United States were being guarded from the awesome power of Kasma in the secret headquarters of the outlaw band known as the Hidden Hundred!

For a long time, there had been no hint of other presences about this secret room. But now the President and the Vice-President sensed strange activities. They heard footfalls above them, movements beyond the walls, curious noises penetrating the floor. They could not know that the members of the Hidden Hundred stationed at this secret rendezvous were taking uncommon means of protecting them.

Orders had flashed over the secret telephone line to *X-66*, in charge. In the rooms surrounding that in which the President and Vice-President were locked, the captain's commands were being carried out. Huge truckloads of insulating material had been brought to the adjoining house and passed into this one through a hidden door in the cellar. Hundreds of heavy paper bags had been ripped open and their fleecy contents removed. This sound-absorbent, snowy stuff was being packed rapidly around the room that contained the leaders of the federal government.

It lay now in a thick layer on the floor of the room above;

it was piled high against all the walls; it was being packed under the floor. Even the conduits of the ventilating system were surrounded with it. The room in which the President and Vice-President were hidden rapidly became a cubicle into which the Hidden Hundred hoped the deadly sound-beam of Kasma could not penetrate, even if the hideaway should somehow be discovered.

In rooms upstairs, other members of the Hidden Hundred were engaged upon another strange task. A heavy consignment of thick, fleecy fabric had also been trucked to the secret headquarters. With it had been brought electric sewing-machines and huge scissors. The Hidden Hundred were tailoring weird garments out of this stuff—heavy robes, thick helmets. Following the orders of their commander, they were making these garments rapidly, after the pattern of that weird costume worn by the unknown Yellowese who had been captured on the Mexican border.

"Those robes are protection against the power of Kasma," Operator 5 had informed the Hidden Hundred. "All of you must be supplied. The lieutenants of the Son of Kasma have no doubt accustomed themselves, through long training, to the effects of the sound-beams, but we cannot hope to do that. Perhaps these robes will not be enough to save you—but it is a gamble we must take."

Sewing-machines hummed; insulating material was still being packed around that one black room; inside it, the President and Vice-President of the United States waited while the passing moments promised the doom of their nation....

157

IN A conference room in the State, War and Navy Building, which stood near the White House, grave-faced men were gathered. They were the highest ranking officers of the Army and Navy, the members of the General Staff. A special message from WDC-13 had called them together; now they waited with raw nerves for the appearance of Z-7 and Operator 5.

Quick steps approached the door. The Washington chief and Jimmy Christopher entered the room quickly. The officers of the Joint Board peered at them for a silent moment, sensing that they were living a momentous episode in the history of their nation. Z-7 broke the silence with his low, throaty voice:

"Gentlemen, I call upon the General Staff to cooperate with our crippled Intelligence to combat the power of Kasma."

Silently he proffered a teletype report to Major-General Falk, Chief of Staff. General Falk's eyes widened as he read. He passed the flimsy to his Deputy. It was read in turn by the Brigadier General in charge of the War-Plans Division, by all the officers of the Joint Board. It was startling information:

...WDC-13... FOLLOWING PREVIOUS REPORT ON MYSTIC CULT DOMINATION OF DROUGHT AREA IN MID-WEST... THE GUARDED DESERT AREA BEING PLACED UNDER EVEN HEAVIER WATCH... NOW AN ISOLATED SECTION COMPLETELY CONTROLLED BY THE MYSTICS... MILLIONS HAVE BEGUN GIGANTIC EXODUS TOWARD KASMA SHRINE... COUNTLESS TERRORIZED FAMILIES THROWING THEMSELVES BEFORE KASMA TO DO

HIS WILL... IMPOSSIBLE FOR OUR FEW AGENTS TO PENETRATE GUARDED DESERT REGION, BUT CERTAIN THAT EXODUS MARKS FIRM ESTABLISH-MENT OF KASMA CULT IN UNITED STATES, AND BEGINNING OF COMPLETE DOMINATION OF NATION BY SON OF KASMA... WE ARE HELPLESS TO STEM TIDE... UNLESS KASMA IS CHECKED NOW NATION IS LOST... TK

The Chief of Staff stared at Z-7. The chief's gesture moved Operator 5 to the head of the table. Jimmy Christopher spoke clearly, softly, forcefully.

"Gentlemen, we must penetrate into the heart of that desert region which is the mecca of these terrorized millions. We must seize the control of it away from the Son of Kasma. We must reveal his awful fakery and send these hysterical people back to their homes. Upon our campaign the destiny of the nation depends. For the success of this move, we need the full strength of our army."

Major-General Falk declared: "The Secretaries of War and Navy have directed me to cooperate with you. We will do our utmost. I will immediately marshal our military force into that area."

"You must remember," Operator 5 pointed out, "that we are, actually, being forced to fight our own people. We *must* turn them back, but we must avoid all possible bloodshed. We must rely on sheer unarmed man-power if possible. If this is not possible—then the lives of a few must pay the cost of saving the entire nation. But at all costs, we must regard that territory as soil seized by a foreign enemy, and we must regain control of it and break the power which has seized it."

JIMMY CHRISTOPHER laid closely written sheets on the table. "With Z-7, I have outlined here a possible strategy, calling for the cooperation of air and land units. Above all, they must approach that territory as quietly, as carefully, as possible. All units must hold themselves ready for a united attack. I hope to be able to give the signal by radio."

"We will destroy that damned army of mystic Orientals, I promise you!"

"If they do not destroy you, first, General Falk."

"What?"

"You are fighting a weapon which you have never before faced," Jimmy Christopher pointed out. "At this moment you have no means of defense against it. Not a moment must be lost in providing yourselves with the necessary protection. This can consist of only one thing—thick garments of sound-absorbent material which will completely cover your men from head to foot."

"You may leave the use of our equipment to me, young man," the Chief of Staff answered frostily. "I have full confidence in our manpower. It will not be necessary to resort to any such grotesque expedient. I will hear no more of this insane idea."

Operator 5's lips pressed hard. The stony expression on the faces of the General Staff convinced him that to argue further was useless. He well knew the resistance of the trained military mind to the acceptance of any unconventional methods. A heavy dread filled his heart as he turned at the opening of a door. The

Secretary of the Joint Board, looking in, declared: "Your plane is waiting at Bolling Field, gentlemen. It is ready to takeoff for New York now."

Operator 5 and Z-7 strode swiftly from the conference room—grave and anxious with the realization that the coming hours must decide the fate of a great nation....

THE GUARDED elevator of Headquarters HN in New York lifted Operator 5 and Z-7 and Tim Donovan to the suite of secret operations-offices. The agent in charge of the Manhattan area, Y-4, rose alertly as they entered. Z-7 asked quickly, his voice crackling:

"Is there a report from the men you have on watch at the Sub-Treasury and the Stock Exchange?"

"Their report, Chief, is still 'all quiet.'"

Operator 5's darkened eyes expressed profound relief. "Have you made the preparations for me, Y-4?"

DURING THEIR swift flight from Washington to Mitchell Field, Jimmy Christopher had wirelessed instructions to HN. He had carefully planned his moves, and these called for the close cooperation of the New York headquarters. Y-4 answered the question with a brisk nod, said:

"The autogyro is ready now, Operator 5. It is in the concealed hangar on the top floor. One of our best army pilots, Lieutenant Crosbie, is waiting there with it, ready to take off at short notice."

"The wireless equipment?"

"Is in the plane, sir, ready—a powerful portable sender and receiver."

"The parachutes?"

"Are also in the plane, ready to be put on."

"Dr. Coombs?"

"Is waiting." Y-4 touched a button on his desk, and a communicating door opened. The big, gray-headed man who entered was the Intelligence surgeon for the Manhattan area. He carried his small case with him and blinked gravely as he shook hands with Operator 5 and Z-7. "You have the serum, doctor?"

"Yes."

"Please come with me." Jimmy Christopher led the way along the corridor, and opened the door of the small space which connected with the cells. In one of them the unknown Yellowese was still held captive—the placid-faced young man of proud bearing who had become the prisoner of the Intelligence at the Mexican border. He rose slowly from a chair as Operator 5 entered the cell, followed by Z-7, Dr. Coombs and Tim Donovan.

Quietly Operator 5 asked: "You remember me?"

The lean yellow face was inscrutable.

"I have come to hear you tell me who you are."

There was no answer.

"I believe," Operator 5 answered, "that it's a fearless trust in the power of Kasma that keeps him silent—though his mind is certainly affected. Doctor—proceed."

Dr. Coombs approached the unknown Yellowese, opened his case. The blank-faced man did not protest when the physician rolled one sleeve high on the thin, saffron arm. With skilled quickness, Dr. Coombs snapped the neck off an ampoule and filled the barrel of a hypodermic syringe. Still the prisoner did not protest when the needle plunged into his flesh, and its contents were slowly discharged.

Dr. Coombs immediately stepped back. Operator 5 took the prisoner's arm, suggested gently: "Lie down, my friend. Rest." Obediently, the Yellowese lowered himself to the cot in the room, and lay lax. His eyes did not close, but a dreaminess came into them. Operator 5 observed the first effects of the drug scopolamine, sometimes called the Truth Serum.

OPERATOR 5 waited for the effects to take full hold on the Yellowese. He realized that the name "Truth Serum" was inaccurate, since the drug did not force the subject to tell the truth; it merely brought out, in spoken words, whatever was uppermost in the numbed mind, whether it was truth or fancy. In spite of this, Jimmy Christopher hoped to learn a secret that might further reveal the ramifications of the amazing plan of the Son of Kasma.

"You feel comfortable, my friend?"

"Yes."

"You are not happy here?"

"I am wretched."

"You wish to go away?"

"I yearn to return to the land of my fathers."

"You left it of your own will?"

"I departed in obedience to a will stronger than mine—the will of Kasma."

"Do you doubt the power of Kasma?"

"No."

"Would you doubt it if you learned that it is not a supernatural power, but a scientific force used by a cult of scheming mystics to enslave the world?"

"If the power of Kasma failed, I should return happily to the faith of my ancestors."

"The power of Kasma is an ugly trickery. It is not worthy of your faith. You will return to your home to honor your ancestors and again be happy."

"That is well."

"We will prove to you that Kasma is a false god, and we will return you safely to your home."

"It is well."

"What is your name, my friend?"

"Hako."

Operator 5 straightened suddenly. His alarmed glance shot to Z-7. The Washington chief stood stunned at the very sound of the name, and his face went pale. Tensely Jimmy Christopher bent over the Yellowese again.

"What is your name?" he repeated.

"Hako."

"And the name of your venerable father?"

"Fusa."

Again Jimmy Christopher straightened. "Rest," he said softly. "Rest...."

He moved from the room, and Z-7 and the others followed. The Washington chief peered at Operator 5's eyes in unbounded astonishment. In a hushed tone he exclaimed:

"That young man is the son of the Yellow Emperor!"

Operator 5 answered tensely: "That explains the consternation reported in the royal court of the Yellow Empire! It shows how far-flung the plan of the Son of Kasma is! Through his followers, he was able to succeed in kidnapping the son of the Yellow Emperor and bring him to the United States!"

"But in God's names—!"

"Do you realize what that means, Chief? The Son of Kasma has not only plotted to seize control of the United States government. He has planned to establish Hako as the figure-head of this country. It is a scheme to spread the cult of Kasma from the United States into the Yellow Empire. That alone will give the Son of Kasma virtual domination of more than half the globe. The most gigantic plan of conquest ever conceived, chief—and its object is to conquer the world and seize its wealth!"

Z-7 declared tightly: "We can thwart that plan by returning Hako to the Yellow Empire—but the danger threatening the United States is still as great."

"Exactly. And unless we can destroy the very roots of the cult of Kasma in this country within the next few hours or days, we will face a hopeless—"

OPERATOR 5 broke off as the door of the communications-room burst open. The chief-dispatcher of HN took long, swift strides to Z-7. His blurted words brought a chilling shock through Jimmy Christopher's heart.

"A report from the men in Wall street, sir! The power is striking again! The Stock Exchange building is beginning to go to pieces! Kasma is destroying it even now!"

Operator 5 spun. He dashed into the elevator cab which was waiting. Tim Donovan kept anxiously at his side; Z-7 shouldered through the panel as it slid shut. "All the way up, fast as you can make it!" Operator 5 commanded, and the car sped. Seconds later the panel widened again, and Jimmy Christopher hurried into the huge room where the autogyro sat.

Orders telephoned by Y-4 had caused the pilot to start the motor. A muffled roar shook the air as Operator 5 hurried to the pit. Lieutenant Crosbie, ace pilot of the Air Corps, signaled readiness as he settled to the controls. Jimmy Christopher sprang over the cowling, snapped: "Take her up!"

A huge electric motor was whirring in one corner of the room: a shaft was revolving and a worm gear was sliding away the steel ceiling. The open sky became visible above, bright blue spotted with fluffy clouds. This device entirely concealed this special platform when it was not in use. Jimmy Christopher waited anxiously for the space to open all the way; and suddenly he was conscious of someone clambering into the pit with him.

Tim Donovan blurted: "I'm going too!"

"Tim, you don't understand! If my plan works out, I won't stay with this plane! You can't—!"

"You can't keep me back, Jimmy!"

Tears glistened in the lad's eyes as his hard hands gripped the cowling. A glance upward told Operator 5 that the folding roof was entirely withdrawn. The motor of the gyro hummed up as the pilot peered back. Operator 5's one arm went tightly across Tim Donovan's shoulder and he smiled. He reached out to Z-7's extended hand.

"God be with you, Operator 5!"

Operator 5 commanded: "Up!"

A SAVAGE, merciless force of disintegration had fallen swiftly upon the famed Stock Exchange building in Wall Street. Nerve-center of the financial organism of industry in the United States, it had been thronged during these hours of feverish trading. At the first crash of doom, terrorized mobs had stampeded into the open. Now Wall Street was a scene of havoc and terror.

The great structure was quaking on its base, crashing to bits, rapidly becoming a mass of ruins. Under tumbled masonry scores lay crushed and dead. All thought of routine business vanished from the minds of those who fled hysterical from the center of destruction. In this street were the offices of great financiers who controlled the destinies of far-flung corporations and of foreign states; but now, their power was being wiped out of existence by the greater power of Kasma.

Dust clouded thickly into air that had a few moments ago been filled with the bright, morning sunshine. It covered the terrorized men and women who fled; it beat into their lungs as they shouted:

"The Son of Kasma was here!" "He pointed his finger and the building began to fall!" "He's gone now—gone!" Higher into the air, blanketing the whole section of the city, the dust of destruction gusted, springing up until it became a huge cloud rolling over the earth.

Far up in its brilliant blue, the autogyro carrying Operator 5 was soaring. His orders to his pilot sent it weaving up against the ceiling, until now it hovered at a point where maneuvering was treacherous. He peered directly down through his powerful binoculars, saw the pall of doom shrouding the spot where the power of Kasma had hurled the silent, invisible bolt.

Clouds lay below him, drifting serenely with the wind. Jimmy Christopher turned his lenses upon them, searching their depths. In all that vast expanse of open air, there was not the slightest sign of any strange craft in flight. His reason told Operator 5 that the force of Kasma must be striking from the sky; yet he saw no clue to the generating source. Grimly, realizing that the passing moments were decreasing his chances of success in this last, desperate gamble, he swung the shaft of his sight farther through the clouds.

"Is it there, Jimmy?" Tim Donovan asked breathlessly.

"Nothing, Tim! Nothing!"

Suddenly the sky quaked. From all around the hovering gyro, the deafening burst of sound beat. It came from nowhere, yet from everywhere—that strange thunderclap in a clear sky which meant that the destructive work of Kasma was completed. The laugh of the destroying god rolled out of space....

It broke into confusing echoes that clattered off into eternity while Operator 5 desperately searched the air below him.

Suddenly he exclaimed: "That's it! That's it!"

Tim, peering overside, could see nothing in that irregular pattern of white fluff floating between them and the earth. Yet Operator 5 was peering with eager concentration to a point almost directly below. His lips curved into a tight smile as he lowered his glasses and pointed.

"There, Tim—see it? That one cloud among all the others.

All except that one are floating with the wind. That one alone is moving *across* the wind-current!"

Tim exclaimed: "I see it, Jimmy!"

"Inside that cloud, then," Operator 5 declared, "is the sky-craft of Kasma. The force struck out of it. It must be an artificially generated cloud made by the dirigible itself—a sort of smoke-screen that can travel with it That's our mark!"

HE TURNED to the goggled pilot and commanded: "Down—carefully! Close to that run-away cloud. Keep directly above it and don't get too near!"

Tim was still peering overside. "You've found it, Jimmy! It's still moving away from the others!"

"That's the answer, Tim." Operator 5 was quickly moving in the pit. "The dirigible carries generators to make that cloud of fog. It must cling around the craft by ionization. Keep watching it Tim. I'm going down there."

"You're going down, Jimmy?" the boy asked, amazed.

Jimmy Christopher was checking the apparatus which had been stored in the pit by Y-4's orders. There were two parachutes: one the regulation pack, the other of gossamer silk folded as a flat, thin envelope. There was also the portable wireless equipment, consisting of two boxes connected by a cable of wires, both fastened to a harness. Jimmy Christopher quickly removed his coat.

He fastened the thin, flat parachute to his back, then replaced his coat. Next he slipped into the harness of the wireless set and strapped it tight. The boxes hung low, one in the small of his back, the other in front at the level of his waist. Next he wriggled into the harness of the regulation 'chute-pack, and tightened the buckles. Tim Donovan watched him wide-eyed as he again peered overside.

"Still directly above, sir," Lieutenant Crosbie shouted back. "Are we low enough?"

"Hold her!" Operator 5 commanded.

He turned to Tim Donovan. "I'm bailing out now, Tim," he said quietly. "You've been with me from the first on this case—you know the dangers we're facing. If anything should happen to me, old-timer—remember you're going into the service as soon as you're old enough, and you're going to be the best operator the Intelligence ever had."

TEARS GLIMMERED in Tim's eyes. "Gee. Jimmy!" he said huskily. "Can't—can't I take the jump with you? If we come through, it'll be all right. But if we don't, it won't make any difference to me, Jimmy. I—I'd rather—Jimmy, if you didn't come back—!"

The boy's hot hand closed on Operator 5's. "Stout fella, Tim," Jimmy Christopher said softly. "It'll be your job to look after Dad and Diane, you know. They'll need you—and the Service, too. Not this trip, old-timer. Chin up!"

Jimmy Christopher's arm tightened across the Irish lad's shoulders. Quickly, then, he lifted himself to the cowling while the gyro hovered. He peered down, saw the cross-drifting cloud directly below him. He took one long, deep breath, felt the cold metal of the rip-cord ring in his fingers—and stepped off into space.

Wind rushed past him as he plunged. One glance showed

him the gyro apparently flying off into empty space above—with Tim Donovan, wide-eyed, peering down at him. A tornado was tearing around him when, at the count of ten, he zipped the rip-cord away. With a smile, he tucked it in his pocket; he heard the snap of the pilot 'chute, then the *poom* of the great silk bell as it snapped tight.

He pendulumed wildly as he floated earthward, while the wind sang through the shroud-lines. Peering down, he saw himself drifting away from the mysterious cloud. Pulling on the shrouds, he spilled air from the 'chute and navigated toward it. He was lowering toward it at an even rate when, swinging wide, he again glanced up toward the autogyro he had left.

Chill amazement filled him—for another parachute was glistening in the sun! A second silken bell had blossomed against the sky and a small figure was dangling in its harness. Tim Donovan! The boy was following Operator 5. He had made use of the 'chute stored under the cubby seat. Jimmy Christopher watched in dismay as the boy drifted downward after him.

Filled with consternation, hoping against hope that the boy would be unable to reach the concealed sky-craft and would descend into a New York street, he again pulled the shroud-lines to throw himself toward the fleecy mass below him. He could not know exactly what it hid. Once he plunged into its depths, his strategy might come to an abrupt and tragic end. Yet now his move was started; it must be carried through. Jimmy Christopher directed himself toward the heart of the floating fog.

Pungent grayness suddenly enveloped Operator 5. The sky and the earth vanished at the same instant. He was surrounded by blinding mist. He could see nothing, but the neutral color of the fog as he continued to float downward through it. Straining his eyes to peer below him, he watched and hoped for a faint sight of something that might reflect the light of the sun. For long, dread moments there was only that acrid gray nothingness around him, until—

A strangely patterned surface appeared dimly. It seemed to expand in Operator 5's gaze until it became an island floating in the sky. Desperately Jimmy Christopher jerked at the shrouds as he dropped close to it. When his feet were dangling near, another sharp pull spurted him downward. Deliberately he flung himself forward as the silken bell fluttered and spilled down near him.

On all sides and above him, the gray mass of fleece hung, sparkling with the iridescent glitter as the sunlight shafted into it. He was resting on his side on a surface which had yielded beneath him—a rubberized fabric patterned into a strange variegation of colors. It extended far in front and behind him, seeming to taper to a point. On the sides, it curved downward, rounding off into the space within the mass of the cloud. Operator 5 realized with a bounding heart that his deduction was true. He had landed on the top of a great dirigible.

A flicker of motion startled him. Peering ahead, he saw a ghostly black movement in the gray. It floated downward, drifted to the varicolored surface, then partly vanished. Over it a flutter of white descended. Operator 5 felt mingled agony and elation as he worked himself along the sagging surface and risked a whispering call: "Tim!"

"Jimmy!" the hushed answer came.

Operator 5 wriggled from the parachute harness, then worked himself toward the spot at which the plucky Irish lad had descended. He saw Tim scrambling up and whispered a word of warning. The boy freed himself of his 'chute and came crawling across the surface. It sloped upward, to form a narrow dividing line, and toward that central spot both Operator 5 and Tim Donovan crawled.

"Jimmy, I had to come!" the boy blurted, and his eyes shone with tears. "I'd rather die with you than stay back. Don't be sore at me!"

Operator 5 smiled tightly. "You're a game lad, old-timer. I'm glad you're here. Having you with me—well, it gives me a feeling that we're going to come through. You're my mascot as well as my partner, aren't you, Tim?"

"Gee, Jimmy!" the boy breathed. "I think you're the swellest guy in the world!"

CHAPTER 11
CITADEL OF EVIL

CONSTANTLY, HOUR after hour, Z-7 remained at his post in the communications-room of HN, awaiting the wireless reports from Operator 5. Following the first electrifying word, came a long period of silence from Operator 5. The Washington chief realized that this was caution on the part of Jimmy Christopher, that he knew he must make his reports infrequently lest they be discovered. Each moment was an agony to the chief until the next report came.

"Operator 5 calling HN! We are in position on top of a craft which appears to be a dirigible. It is flying at an even speed, westward and a little south. By this time, it has already passed out of the zone of the principal eastern cities, though I can see nothing from my position. There is good reason to believe the craft is heading toward the Mid-Western region which the Son of Kasma commands."

Z-7's voice crackled into the microphone. "In God's name, Operator 5, safeguard yourself in every possible way!"

"We are safe right now. No one knows we're here…. Chief, is there any report on the Secretary and Diane?"

"None!"

Again there was a long period of anxious silence in the ether, while Z-7 waited in HN. He could not think of rest or his many other duties; Jimmy Christopher's momentous strategy was his whole concern.

Day was dying when, at last, Z-7 was galvanized by the sound of Operator 5's voice issuing again from the loudspeaker.

"Calling HN! This craft is still proceeding on its course. Its destination is certainly that section which the Son of Kasma has seized. Our report must be right. This voyage and the exodus from the drought region, means that the mystic cult intends to root itself into our soil swiftly."

Z-7 asked quickly: "You are still safe?"

"All safe, Chief. Still no report on the Secretary and Diane? What word from the Chief of Staff?"

"The Secretary and Diane are still lost. Word has just been received from General Staff that mobilization is under way. Troops are moving toward the seized area now. All air units are moving up. They will wait at their appointed stations until you sound the signal to close in. You may depend upon absolute cooperation."

"Stand by, Chief!"

EVENING FELL while Z-7 continued to wait. Darkness deepened slowly. The westward movement of the strange craft, the chief knew, was prolonging its period of daylight while it traveled with the sun. Two hours after night had fallen upon New York City, another radio report flashed out of the ether.

"Calling HN! The craft is descending! It is slowly going down under cover of darkness. The apparatus which generates the cloud-screen has ceased to function, and we are lowering now through clear air. As far as I can see, we are in a region of flat, open country. We are still descending."

Z-7 questioned: "Do you think this is your destination, Operator 5?"

"I doubt it, Chief. We have not yet crossed the Mississippi. Wait! There is an airplane descending! It is coming down close to us! We may be sighted!"

Sharp agony pinched at Z-7's heart as he waited. With agonizing vividness, he could picture the scene which Jimmy Christopher's few words implied: two small figures clinging to the back of the sky-monster. A plane soaring over and around them while they crouched without being able to hide themselves.

175

"Chief!" came through the crackling ether, "the plane is landing. Perhaps we were seen, but I think not. It is dark enough so that we stood a chance of being unseen. The dirigible is floating low over the ground. The motors are off. Apparently this is a secret landing-field, for the movement of this craft indicates that it is being towed by men on the ground. We have come down."

Another tense period; then the clear voice of Operator 5 resumed:

"We are ascending once more! The engines are again functioning, and we are climbing rapidly. The course is the same as before. There is only one conclusion, Chief. The craft went down to pick up passengers brought by the plane. It's possible that the Son of Kasma has come aboard this ship!"

"Go on, Operator 5!"

The period of silence that followed was more prolonged than any of the previous ones. Z-7 paced back and forth in the communications-room of HN while a technician remained on constant duty at the board. Any thought of sleep was intolerable to him. Though Y-4 urged him to rest, he could not. He kept listening to the faint crackle of static that came from the loud speaker, hoping to hear again the hum of the carrier-wave which would mean that a new report was coming. But an endless, agonized period passed before the voice of Operator 5 again spoke out of the ether.

"Calling HN! Operator 5 calling HN! Again the craft is descending! We are flying now above the dust-storm region, and I am sure that the stronghold of Kasma is somewhere below.

Immediately I become certain that the ship is going to land, I will make my next move, Chief. Stand by!"

THE HUM of the carrier continued. Z-7 dared not speak for fear his own voice would drown out Operator 5's next words. Bent tensely before the loud-speaker, he waited breathlessly until:

"Calling HN! It is impossible to see what lies directly beneath us, both because of the ship and the darkness. We cannot remain on board longer if this is the end of the voyage—but if it is not, we will be left behind, and it will mean the failure of this whole move."

Far out in the thick darkness that blanketed the nation. Operator 5 spoke the decisive words into the transmitter. Now he clicked the switch off and peered at Tim Donovan. The darkness was so thick that he could scarcely see the boy crouching near him. They were worn by the long strain of their precarious voyage; their hunger was a sharp pain and their thirst burned their throats. Yet the momentous significance of the moment made them unconscious of all else.

"Tim, old-timer," Operator 5 said quietly, "we're going back toward the tail. Watch me—slide off when I do. You know how to manage a 'chute in the air. Stay as close to me as possible. If anything should happen to me, Tim, and you keep clear, then by all means use this transmitter and keep Z-7 informed."

The boy steadied himself, pressing his lips tightly. "Okay, Jimmy," he said tersely. "I'll do my best."

They turned together, began to crawl over the camouflaged back of the great sky craft. During the long, trying journey they had folded and re-packed their parachutes. The bundles were again harnessed to their backs. Through the darkness, as the tremendous ship descended, they worked their way toward the tail. The wind soughed past them as they huddled on the tilted back of the craft and made ready.

"Down as far as you can, Tim," Operator 5 directed softly. "Then go over."

Jimmy Christopher went flat on the camouflaged surface; Tim stretched out beside him. They wriggled down the curve of the back of the dirigible. The craft was still descending; wind soughed past it. Lower and lower Operator 5 and the boy worked themselves over the sloping fabric. Suddenly Tim gasped; he slid downward at quickening speed. Immediately Operator 5 thrust himself after the boy.

The surface vanished in front of them: they dropped into empty air, glimpsing one of the gondolas of the craft, with its spinning propellers, as they fell. Lights twinkled on the underside of the sky monster and streaked above them. Operator 5 ripped his pack open, and the parachute flicked out. He jerked in the shrouds and swung, peering around. In the darkness near him he saw Tim Donovan hovering, and a sigh of relief passed his lips.

Above them, the dirigible floated, sliding downward, its nose dipped. Below spread unseen ground. For long moments Operator 5 and Tim Donovan drifted; and suddenly their hearts were frozen by an unforeseen danger.

LIGHT GLARED below them! A bright shine sprang over the ground. Peering down, Jimmy Christopher saw the land-

Within the scarlet walls, the Son of Kasma spoke: "Turn the power on them!"

179

ing crew waiting—a swarm of tiny figures. Instantly he pulled at the shrouds of his 'chute and gasped a call to Tim to follow his example. Wind spilled from the silken bells, and they slid sharply through the air. The quick maneuver sent them downward at a sharp angle, away from the glare of light.

A torture of anxiety filled them as they drifted. Had they been seen? Operator 5 did not know; he continued to navigate away from the shine, with Tim Donovan swinging nearby. Ground, faintly grayed with light, blurred beneath them. Their swinging feet touched. They fell flat, dragging at the shroud-lines, flattening their 'chutes. Breathless they lay on the dusty ground, peering toward the dirigible.

The landing crew was mobbing beneath it, pulling the ropes it had lowered. It was dipping into a hollow in the ground. Operator 5 saw that the tremendous hangar of the craft had been excavated beneath the surface; its roof was a dome of dust-heaped earth. Without moving, Jimmy Christopher and Tim Donovan lay side by side, until the gigantic craft slid slowly into the hollow and vanished from sight.

They had landed, they knew, within the guarded precincts of the desert region seized upon by the Son of Kasma. While the lights still burned they glimpsed, in the distance, a tremendous edifice that had been built in the center of the dry, dust—covered area. They looked upon the scarlet walls and the looming facade of a temple erected to Kasma in the wasteland.

Farther off in the gloom, almost invisible, Operator 5 discerned towers rearing. The giant steel spires rose far into the night sky. Topping them were huge platforms. On each of the platforms were gigantic parabolic reflectors. Around them, puny in comparison, men were standing. Jimmy Christopher realized that tremendously powerful dynamic speakers were enclosed in these reflectors—that from the pinnacles of the towers the deadly beams could be shot to cover every approach.

Grimly he clicked the switch of the radio equipment. When the tubes warmed, be whispered into the microphone: "Calling GS! Calling GS!"

The voice that answered was that of the Chief of Staff. Somewhere out in the desert night, he was waiting with his officers. His words came huskily: "GS on your wave!"

"Stand by for the signal!"

Operator 5 trimmed the oscillator to a different band. Again he spoke rapidly into the microphone: "Calling X-13!"

Out of the night came another whisper. "X-13 answering!" The voice was that of John Christopher. The orders of the captain of the Hidden Hundred had dispatched the outlawed agents to scattered points surrounding the guarded area. They had found their way into this territory by private plane during the long day; now their commander was speaking through the night:

"Stand by for the signal!"

OPERATOR 5 stopped short, peering at the mouth of the hollow into which the great dirigible had crawled. Figures were walking into the open. Leading them with slow, majestic stride was a lean, tall man garbed in scarlet robe and scarlet turban. He moved through the night like a crimson ghost—the Son of Kasma!

Jimmy Christopher saw the lieutenants of the mystic, all black-robed Yellowese, following their master. Among the Orientals walked a man and a girl. Operator 5's heart speeded as he recognized the Secretary of State and Diane Elliot. Led by the Son of Kasma, surrounded by the black-cloaked lieutenants, the Secretary and the girl were led toward a smaller building which stood not far from the tremendous tabernacle erected to Kasma in the desert.

Operator 5 waited anxiously until the procession passed from sight within the scarlet structure. The landing-crew hurried out of the shine of light; and suddenly the gleam vanished. Utter darkness filled the guarded area, except at one point far across the desert of dust. Peering in that direction, Jimmy Christopher saw multitudes of people massing toward the temple.

They were a continual parade, coming out of the night, following well-tramped roads which radiated through the wasteland. Jimmy Christopher realized that thousands of them had already entered the temple, that thousands more would follow them, that others would mass into this area of evil sanctuary until millions clustered around the citadel of Kasma. The exodus was at its height. Kasma was claiming this multitude for his own; his power was soon to spread from coast to coast to dominate the United States.

Now the windows of the temple gleamed with scarlet light. From its interior, the strains of weird music played—the same toneless, rhythm-less melody that Operator 5 had heard in the hidden temple in New York City. The spell of Kasma was playing over the devout who had come to kneel in obeisance, and the great scarlet windows of the temple spread their evil light across the desert.

Operator 5 moved quickly, signaling Tim Donovan to follow, toward the smaller scarlet structure into which the Son of Kasma had led the procession from the dirigible. When he came near, he moved with the utmost caution. In this building, as in the tabernacle crimson windows glowed. Jimmy Christopher crept close to one of them, then to another. He paused when he heard a guttural voice say:

"The will of the Son of Kasma is that they be held prisoner here. The man will become the instrument of our rule. The girl will spread the word of the Son of Kasma across the nation through the great news distributing system which she serves. They will wait until the son of Kasma has disclosed his will."

OPERATOR 5 tightened suddenly as a muffled drone sounded in the air above him. Peering up, he sensed a fluttering of wings, but he could see nothing. The drone grew louder; abruptly a glare again spread out of the darkness. Operator 5 and Tim Donovan flattened frantically against the scarlet wall, peered at the glistening wings of a descending plane.

It swooped to the ground, and immediately the lights blinked out. Excited, guttural voices followed, drawing nearer. Men were running toward the house of Kasma's son. Operator 5 glimpsed one, in the scarlet glow of the windows, leading the way. He was a Yellowese, garbed in pilot's uniform. He burst through the entrance of the small, red building, and Jimmy Christopher heard his ringing voice give a report.

"The Son of Kasma must know that our citadel is surrounded

by those who oppose us! Many men in the uniform of the United States army are waiting. They have fast cars and airplanes hidden out in the night!… Master! We are in danger!"

Operator 5 sensed the appearance of the Son of Kasma before the pilot. There was a moment of silence within the scarlet walls. Then, in his low, whispering voice, the Son of Kasma spoke:

"Kasma does not fear them. Kasma will destroy them. Obey his will! Turn the power upon the doomed!"

Quickly, his blood rushing, Operator 5 clicked the switch of the portable wireless unit. In agony he waited until the tubes warmed. He pressed the microphone close to his lips and whispered: "Calling GS! Calling GS!"

"GS on your wave!"

"Attack!"

Swiftly, Operator 5 trimmed the oscillator to the waveband of the field equipment of the Hidden Hundred. Again his whisper shot through the night, out into the desert: "Calling X-13! Calling X-13!"

"X-13 picking you up. Captain!"

"Attack! Attack!"

The moment when the destiny of the United States must be decided had come…!

CHAPTER 12
UNHOLY CITY

O UT IN the depths of the darkness, the crackling commands of officers whipped the waiting infantry into action.

"Forward!"

Thousands of men in the uniform of the United States army had been awaiting the signal. Now they sped forward from their hidden stations, following orders already outlined to them.

Farther out on the fields of black, still other commands were relayed by tight-nerved officers from the wireless field units which had been waiting for this galvanizing order.

"Take off!"

Motors snarled. Their wings spreading over the desert dust, scores of fast planes of the Air Corps had been waiting. The skilled pilots detailed to this desperate mission had been tensed impatiently at their sticks. Now, as power plants surged, as propellers slashed the night, fat tires rolled over the blanketing dust. Singing a song of defiance, the battle-birds of the Army soared into the night sky.

Between the roads, the infantry advanced through choking clouds of dust. The barking commands of officers sent them driving through scattering mobs who fled from the roads. Rifles ready, they hurried their line toward the Yellowese sentries which they knew were waiting.

And out of the darkness strange figures came rushing. They seemed like inhuman monsters to the crowds who fled the roads

185

in terror. They were enormously fat; their arms were amazingly thick; their heads were huge, fungoid growths resting on great broad shoulders. Out of those heads, eyes gleamed in the depths of deep sockets. Above the uncanny eyes, each of these grotesque creatures was marked with a strange symbol—a white skull.

Joining in the attack by land and air, their weird army hurried forward—the Hidden Hundred!

Counter-attack!

To the pinnacles of each of the towers surrounding the scarlet tabernacle, the command of the Son of Kasma flashed. The crews of Yellowese went into quick action. Saffron hands threw giant knife-switches. Men crowded to the helms of the control units which could swing the giant parabolic reflectors to any angle.

INSIDE THE control booths on each tower, Yellowese lieutenants of the Son of Kasma had placed great red records on spinning turntables. Tremendously powerful amplifiers shot the vibrant impulses into the tremendous voice-coils of the monster speakers. From the peak of each of the towers, the beams played—inaudible, invisible shafts which struck death, terror, madness, lethargy into the advancing ranks.

One of the officers' cars speeding toward the temple suddenly swerved from the road. The driver, slumped over the wheel unconscious, sent it plunging. It lurched into thick dust, crunched to a stop, swayed onto its side. The men inside it lay piled on each other, inert—lifeless. The death-beam of the Son of Kasma had struck doom upon them instantly.

Among the ranks of the infantry advancing across the dust

plains, another terrifying force struck. Uniformed men suddenly shrieked, flung their rifles aside. They tore at their clothing, ripped at their hair, glared around bereft of their senses. The snapping commands of their officers gave way to frantic, hysterical screams. They went running wildly, blindly, through the night, howling, gibbering, choking, screaming—scores transformed into ranting maniacs by the power of Kasma!

A power as deadly shot through the sky. The pilots of the planes, driving toward the gleaming red windows of the temple, were suddenly enveloped with a leaden lethargy. Their tenseness vanished; their determination disappeared; they became beings unwilling to move, unable to think. The smart formations soaring across the night sky wavered and broke. Planes brushed together. Their wings crackled and locked. Across all the winged force this devastating apathy played—and planes dropped from the sky like birds wounded in flight!

Yet throughout this area made deadly by the power of Kasma, the weird, fat figures of the Hidden Hundred advanced. Entirely enveloped by the absorbent garments, protected from the supersonic impulses by the soft stuff covering them, they were able to penetrate far toward the red shine of the temple windows. Scores of these weird, black creatures, each marked by the sign of the skull, charged upon the citadel of evil!

The grim Yellowese on the tower platforms turned their cones upon them—and they did not halt. The tremendous horns beat out their deadly forces—and the Hidden Hundred kept advancing. In thickly gloved hands, they gripped automatics and grenades. They swarmed past sentries with spitting guns, herded toward the base of the towers, and launched an attack in desperate defiance of the power of Kasma.

From their fat hands, grenades twirled toward the peaks of the towers. Blasting explosions rocked the platforms. Savage power tore at the control huts, toppled the terrified crews off into space. Mangled bodies dropped into the dust while other Yellowese rushed to the switches. The rocking explosions interrupted the beams of Kasma, but from other towers destructive shafts still turned on the Hidden Hundred as the strange men swarmed deeper into the evil territory.

AGAIN AND again the cracking grenades of the Hidden Hundred blasted tearing power across the platforms. A blinding explosion rocked directly inside one of the giant horns, and it toppled from its base—destroyed. Silent and desperate, the men in the thick garments continued their desperate onslaught, climbing the ladders to the platforms even as they attacked. From all quarters they ran, besieging the alien mystics as all the forces of the infantry and the Air Corps could not do. The cones on the towers swung quickly, over the area around the tabernacle as the Yellow crews attempted to mow down the Hidden Hundred—vainly!

The numbing power of Kasma played around the small scarlet house beside which Operator 5 and Tim Donovan had huddled. Dimly, through the walls, Operator 5 heard a guttural voice exclaim: "We cannot stop them, Master! Our power has no effect upon them!"

And the whispered voice of the Son of Kasma answered: "They will be torn limb from limb by the faithful. They cannot survive the fury of Kasma's children. Soon they will be over-whelmed. First Kasma must wipe out—destroy completely—all who are unprotected against his force. When they have all been killed or driven mad, then these protected beings will be surrounded by Kasma's devout and themselves destroyed! We will strike from the sky with our strongest power!"

Still Operator 5 remained motionless, helpless in the numb-ing power. He sensed movements, saw figures hurrying from the scarlet house. These Yellowese trained to feel no effect from the paralytic beams, moved swiftly while Operator 5 was able only to watch. Tim Donovan's eyes widened in terror while the Son of Kasma, his black-cloak lieutenants at his side, hurried toward the great underground hangar of the dirigible.

Jimmy Christopher realized that once it soared above this area of conflict, all the attack of the army would be completely disrupted. In the darkness surrounding the temple, infantrymen were still struggling to advance. In the sky, a few planes were still flying, striving to reach the power towers for a bomb attack. Yet these men and these planes must meet inevitable doom once the greatest power of Kasma struck—a force stronger than any now beating from the tower cones. Even now, the dirigible was creeping from its underground hangar to turn that terrible doom upon the earth!

AS BEAMS intercrossed, adding their strength to each other, Operator 5 and Tim Donovan were stopped completely. Held absolutely powerless, transformed into unthinking, unfeeling statues, they could only watch the great dirigible crawl into the open. Its crew drew it clear. Its propellers slashed in the scarlet light. A surge of power shook it while it moved more swiftly, rising. The great monster lifted swiftly, circling up, driving into the darkness toward the point from which it could spew with death and madness and havoc over the desert.

Now, as the floating carrier of doom soared, the power that paralyzed Operator 5 diminished. Shifting beams decreased the numbing effect. Again, desperately, with all his strength, he forced himself across the open. Tim Donovan struggled beside him. It was as though they were walking through thick oil. As he fought his way, Operator 5's dull eyes fixed upon a plane that was sitting near the hollow.

Its pilot had brought the alarm of the waiting attackers to the Son of Kasma. It was sitting where it had landed, with prop still idling over, its pit empty. Operator 5 grimly brought his automatic into his hand as he summoned all his strength in a move toward it.

Suddenly the numbing power vanished. The attack of the Hidden Hundred upon towers at the opposite end of the field had turned the concerted beams away from the hollow. With hysterical joy at feeling the freedom of motion, Jimmy Christopher raced toward the plane. "Jimmy!" called from Tim Donovan's lips desperately as Operator 5 clambered into the pit. The motor roared as the boy sped. The wings quaked and slashed the air at the instant Tim's hand clutched the cowling.

Wind howled past the boy as he strove to rise; but he could not. His grip tore loose, and he plunged to the ground. The stunning force rolled him over and over in the dust. He sprang up with tears streaking his blackened face, peering into the glaring, red light. Operator 5 was hurtling the plane upward through the sky at top speed.

The numbing force seized Jimmy Christopher at that instant, even as he climbed.

Desperately, with all the strength he could summon, Jimmy Christopher handled the controls to hurl the plane higher into the sky. His teeth bared with the effort; his heart trip-hammered; his lungs burned with hot breath. Struggling as he had never struggled before, he kept the plane climbing, and peered across the black sky at the floating dirigible. It was swinging now to a spot directly above the red-shining tabernacle—preparing to strike its devastating blow.

On its underside, Operator 5 saw the great horn of the parabolic power-generator. It was swinging directly behind the gondola. Past the lighted windows, Jimmy Christopher saw the red-robed figure of the Son of Kasma. One hand of the Yellowese was gesturing; he was giving orders to sweep the earth with the death-dealing beam. With a frantic effort, Operator 5 kicked his crate around and sent it hurtling toward the great craft.

DELIBERATELY, HE flung the plane above the dirigible. He whirled through the blackness and saw, dimly, the varicolored back of the monster directly below. He pushed the stick forward and sent the ship plunging. While the dread power was still upon him, he forced himself from the seat, stood erect in the tearing wind. Watching the shape of the dirigible grow larger directly ahead of his slashing prop, he struggled to remove his coat.

Breath stopped, heart pounding, he gripped the cowling and

The plane, crashing into the dirigible,

ripped the great gas envelope, causing a terrific explosion!

193

dragged himself over. He hung an instant, then dropped. The wings slashed above him as he plunged through the darkness. He glimpsed the ship driving down, itself a hurtling power, upon the back of the craft. Falling, he struck the sloping side of fabric, and bounded off into space. At that instant he heard a sharp ripping, a muffled explosion—and blinding with flames glared in the sky...!

Operator 5 felt a sudden slackening of the numbing power as he reached for the rip-cord of the special, gossamer silk 'chute. He dragged the ring; the great bell flipped out and flattened. Floating in the air, Jimmy Christopher peered across space, saw great plumes of flame leaping from the very heart of the dirigible. The plane crashing into it had ripped the great gas envelopes, exploding hydrogen had sent a shock of doom through the craft.

Even while Operator 5 watched, floating downward, another tearing concussion shook the craft. It was falling rapidly, a great thing of flames. Its plunge was carrying it into the black desert of dust as white heat consumed it. A delirious joy filled Operator 5 as he watched it hurtle to earth far beyond the red-windowed tabernacle.

His feet struck, and he was dragged along. He pulled himself up frantically, wriggling out of the 'chute-harness, as he heard a call: "Jimmy!" Tim Donovan was rushing toward him. The boy caught at his hand and sobbed.

"Okay, Tim!" Operator 5 reassured him, as he peered around.

He saw the strange, fat figures of the Hidden Hundred moving in a body across the open space around the tabernacle. His glance upward, at the platforms, showed him that the great cones were broken, the power vanquished. From all around in the darkness came the shouts of infantry advancing now with no fiendish power to turn against them. The Hidden Hundred, fleeing through the darkness, swarmed around the red house of the Son of Kasma; then were gone....

Out of the door of the scarlet house, two figures hurried. Operator 5 sprang toward him. The Secretary of State stood spellbound, peering around. Diane Elliot rushed breathless to Operator 5, flung her arms about him. She sobbed in a delirium of joy as Jimmy Christopher held her close. The Secretary peered in distress and bewilderment, ejaculated: "In God's name, how did I get here? What has happened? What does this mean?"

Operator 5 peered across the black ground now swarming with the uniformed men of the infantry. Leaping flames were licking over the twisted wreckage of the dirigible. Its gondola and huge cone were crushed and broken. Within that raging furnace, Operator 5 knew, the Son of Kasma had perished.

"It means, sir," Operator 5 answered the Secretary's bewildered questions grimly, "that the laughter of Kasma is forever silenced!"

THE VOICE of the President of the United States carried across the nation, over a coast-to-coast hook-up, as he spoke quietly in his study in the White House.

"Let us never again be blinded, my friends. We have learned the truth, and let us profit by it. Our eyes are turned into a bright future and we shall reap its promises. May God bless every one of you."

He turned from the microphone, smiled at the men who were

facing him. The Secretary of State, Z-7, and Operator 5 had listened to his address to reassure the nation. Jimmy Christopher clasped his hand tightly when he offered it.

"All thanks to you, Operator 5," he said earnestly.

Z-7 spoke slowly, solemnly: "Mr. President, the Secretary and I, as the chief officers of the Intelligence, have conferred on an important matter. We wish your permission to act upon our decision at once. Mr. Secretary...."

The head of the State Department glanced keenly at Operator 5. "It is due only to the organization known as the Hidden Hundred, Mr. President, that we were able to destroy the power of Kasma. They risked disaster in order to serve their country even while they were being hunted under my orders. I have withdrawn those orders.

"Further, I wish to relinquish my command of the Intelligence to Z-7, and I ask your approval of his plan to call back into the service all the men I so unwisely discharged from it."

"My approval?" the President repeated. "You have it, with all my heart! Reinstate those men! Call them back at once! We may never learn the name of the man who led them so ably—but to them and to him we owe a profound gratitude."

A slow smile curved the lips of Operator 5....

IN A black room, hidden far from the Capitol, there was silence. A dim light, springing out of the darkness, illumined a figure who stood near a table. His head was a skull, his hands were bony claws. Facing him stood rank upon rank of men who were similarly disguised. After a moment of silence, the captain of the Hidden Hundred spoke gently:

"Comrades, our work is at an end. Your service to our cause has been complete and inspiring. I am proud to have worked with you. I am glad that we will no longer be hunted outlaws, that we will again return to the service we love. We have faced death together, comrades. Let us never forget that bond.

"And let me now, gladly and yet regretfully, speak the words that must be our last good-bye.

"Dismiss!"

The light faded. The captain of the Hidden Hundred vanished in the gloom. That darkness wiped out the danger which had menaced these men, brought them to the end of their outlaw activities, and left them covered with glory....

THE FINGER of Operator 5 touched the call-button of the penthouse of a staid apartment-building in the East Sixties in New York. He had approached this door by means which carefully covered him from any possible watcher. He was perfectly garbed; his lips were curved with contentment. Again he touched the button which was inscribed *Carleton Victor;* a manservant opened the door.

"Good evening, Mr. Victor," said Crowe, gentlemen's gentleman extraordinary.

Crowe did not suspect that the identity of Carleton Victor, world-famous photo-portraitist, was a convenient cover for the activities of America's undercover ace. Discreet, efficient, a paragon among man-servants, Crowe considered his master to be a great artist and served him proudly. He took Victor's hat and stick and coat and bowed.

"Has anything of importance come up while I've been away, Crowe?"

"No, sir," Crowe answered. "Nothing whatever, sir."

Victor settled into an easy chair with a sigh. "You didn't, by any chance, Crowe, feel a temptation to yield to Kasma?"

"I beg pardon, sir?" Crowe asked. "I don't quite understand. If I may ask, sir—what is a kasma?"

"What! 'What is a'—!" Victor stared in amazement. "I simply cannot remember, Crowe, that you never read the newspapers. You don't, do you?"

"Never, sir," Crowe admitted with dignity. "I never read the newspapers."

"Then let the matter drop," Victor said. He glanced up again. "What's the matter, Crowe? Why do you look so woeful?"

Crowe's thin nose twitched. "I beg your pardon, sir, but there are times when even I grow restless. I am proud to serve you, sir—I consider it a privilege—yet, on occasion, I yearn to escape the routine, if I may say so. There are times, sir—" the look in Crowe's eyes was as desperate as any Victor had ever seen—" when I wish something exciting would happen."

Very quietly Victor said "I see, Crowe. You wish something exciting would happen?"

"Yes, sir," Crowe said regretfully, as he turned away, and he added, as Victor's smiling eyes followed him: "But nothing ever does."

THE SPIDER

❑	#1: The Spider Strikes	$13.95
❑	#2: The Wheel of Death	$13.95
❑	#3: Wings of the Black Death	$13.95
❑	#4: City of Flaming Shadows	$13.95
❑	#5: Empire of Doom!	$13.95
❑	#6: Citadel of Hell	$13.95
❑	#7: The Serpent of Destruction	$13.95
❑	#8: The Mad Horde	$13.95
❑	#9: Satan's Death Blast	$13.95
❑	#10: The Corpse Cargo	$13.95
❑	#11: Prince of the Red Looters	$13.95
❑	#12: Reign of the Silver Terror	$13.95
❑	#13: Builders of the Dark Empire	$13.95
❑	#14: Death's Crimson Juggernaut	$13.95
❑	#15: The Red Death Rain	$13.95
❑	#16: The City Destroyer	$13.95
❑	#17: The Pain Emperor	$13.95
❑	#18: The Flame Master	$13.95
❑	#19: Slaves of the Crime Master	$13.95
❑	#20: Reign of the Death Fiddler	$13.95
❑	#21: Hordes of the Red Butcher	$13.95
❑	#22: Dragon Lord of the Underworld	$13.95
❑	#23: Master of the Death-Madness	$13.95
❑	#24: King of the Red Killers	$13.95
❑	#25: Overlord of the Damned	$13.95
❑	#26: Death Reign of the Vampire King	$13.95
❑	#27: Emperor of the Yellow Death	$13.95
❑	#28: The Mayor of Hell	$13.95
❑	#29: Slaves of the Murder Syndicate	$13.95
❑	#30: Green Globes of Death	$13.95
❑	#31: The Cholera King	$13.95
❑	#32: Slaves of the Dragon	$13.95
❑	***NEW:*** #33: Legions of Madness	$13.95

THE MYSTERIOUS WU FANG

❑	#1: The Case of the Six Coffins	$12.95
❑	#2: The Case of the Scarlet Feather	$12.95
❑	#3: The Case of the Yellow Mask	$12.95
❑	#4: The Case of the Suicide Tomb	$12.95
❑	#5: The Case of the Green Death	$12.95
❑	#6: The Case of the Black Lotus	$12.95
❑	#7: The Case of the Hidden Scourge	$12.95

G-8 AND HIS BATTLE ACES

❑	#1: The Bat Staffel	$13.95

CAPTAIN SATAN

❑	#1: The Mask of the Damned	$13.95
❑	#2: Parole for the Dead	$13.95
❑	#3: The Dead Man Express	$13.95
❑	#4: A Ghost Rides the Dawn	$13.95
❑	#5: The Ambassador From Hell	$13.95

THE SECRET 6

❑	1: The Red Shadow	$13.95
❑	#2: House of Walking Corpses	$13.95
❑	#3: The Monster Murders	$13.95
❑	***NEW:*** #4: The Golden Alligator	$13.95

CAPTAIN ZERO

❑	#1: City of Deadly Sleep	$13.95
❑	#2: The Mark of Zero!	$13.95
❑	#3: The Golden Murder Syndicate	$13.95

OPERATOR 5

❑	#1: The Masked Invasion	$13.95
❑	#2: The Invisible Empire	$13.95
❑	#3: The Yellow Scourge	$13.95
❑	#4: The Melting Death	$13.95
❑	#5: Cavern of the Damned	$13.95
❑	#6: Master of Broken Men	$13.95
❑	#7: Invasion of the Dark Legions	$13.95
❑	#8: The Green Death Mists	$13.95
❑	#9: Legions of Starvation	$13.95
❑	#10: The Red Invader	$13.95
❑	#11: The League of War-Monsters	$13.95
❑	#12: The Army of the Dead	$13.95
❑	#13: March of the Flame Marauders	$13.95
❑	#14: Blood Reign of the Dictator	$13.95
❑	#15: Invasion of the Yellow Warlords	$13.95
❑	#16: Legions of the Death Master	$13.95
❑	#17: Hosts of the Flaming Death	$13.95
❑	#18: Invasion of the Crimson Death Cult	$13.95

DUSTY AYRES AND HIS BATTLE BIRDS

❑	#1: Black Lightning!	$13.95
❑	#2: Crimson Doom	$13.95
❑	#3: The Purple Tornado	$13.95
❑	#4: The Screaming Eye	$13.95
❑	#5: The Green Thunderbolt	$13.95
❑	#6: The Red Destroyer	$13.95
❑	#7: The White Death	$13.95
❑	#8: The Black Avenger	$13.95
❑	#9: The Silver Typhoon	$13.95
❑	#10: The Troposphere F-S	$13.95
❑	#11: The Blue Cyclone	$13.95
❑	#12: The Tesla Raiders	$13.95

DR. YEN SIN

❑	#1: Mystery of the Dragon's Shadow	$12.95
❑	#2: Mystery of the Golden Skull	$12.95
❑	#3: Mystery of the Singing Mummies	$12.95

MAVERICKS

❑	#1: Five Against the Law	$12.95
❑	#2: Mesquite Manhunters	$12.95
❑	#3: Bait for the Lobo Pack	$12.95
❑	#4: Doc Grimson's Outlaw Posse	$12.95
❑	#5: Charlie Parr's Gunsmoke Cure	$12.95

www.ingramcontent.com/pod-product-compliance
Lightning Source LLC
Chambersburg PA
CBHW020424180626
46812CB00003B/1147